07-BYW-071

D0448603

Why

Winn

The Secret

#16

The Secret Tunnel Mystery

Hilda Stahl

CROSSWAY BOOKS • WHEATON, ILLINOIS
A DIVISION OF GOOD NEWS PUBLISHERS

Dedicated with love to
Vera Stahl

The Secret Tunnel Mystery

Copyright © 1992 by Word Spinners, Inc.

Published by Crossway Books
  a division of Good News Publishers
  1300 Crescent Street
  Wheaton, Illinois 60187

All rights reserved. No part of this publication may be reproduced, stored in a retrieval system or transmitted in any form by any means, electronic, mechanical, photocopy, recording or otherwise, without the prior permission of the publisher, except as provided by USA copyright law.

Cover illustration: Paul Casale

First printing, 1992 (as Best Friends Special Edition); first printing as Best Friends #16, 1994

Printed in the United States of America

Library of Congress Cataloging-in-Publication Data
Stahl, Hilda.
    The secret tunnel mystery / Hilda Stahl.
        p.   cm. — (Best Friends #16)
    Summary: The Best Friends try to solve a dangerous mystery involving hidden tunnels, secret rooms, stolen antiques, and a family too scared to go home.
    [1. Mystery and detective stories.   2. Christian life—Fiction.]
I. Title.   II. Series: Stahl, Hilda. Best Friends special edition : #1.
PZ7.S78244Sb 1992   [Fic]—dc20   92-27202
ISBN 0-89107-826-6

02		01		00		99		98		97		96		95		94
15	14	13	12	11	10	9	8	7	6	5	4	3	2	1

Contents

1

The Shadowy Image

Her eyes wide in alarm, Roxie Shoulders gripped Chelsea McCrea's freckled arm before she could leave the gravel driveway. A warm October wind blew red and gold leaves across the newly mowed lawn of the empty house. Canadian geese honked overhead in the bright blue sky. "Don't go any closer! I don't like the feel of it!"

Kathy Aber and Hannah Shigwam looked at Roxie and laughed.

"You're kidding, of course," Chelsea said in her Oklahoma accent.

"It's beautiful—almost a mansion!" Kathy gazed longingly at the house. She was glad she'd come. If she could, she'd stay even for Sunday so she wouldn't have to be home for the special Sunday visitor and the dinner they were having for him.

"This is better than being at home all day," Hannah said. They had a long week-end because of teachers' conferences. Spending Friday and Saturday in the country was a lot better than listening to Baby Burke cry or hearing the noise her little sisters made. Hannah pushed her hands deep into the front pockets of her jeans. Of course the real reason she was glad to be gone had nothing to do with her sisters and brother—it had to do with Mom's special glass pickle dish that was over a hundred years old. Hannah had accidentally dropped and broken it, and Mom thought the twins did it. Hannah bit back a moan. She'd let Mom blame the twins! That was like telling a lie. And she didn't lie—not ever! Abruptly Hannah pushed the thoughts away and looked at Roxie again.

Roxie shook her head hard as she stared at the two-story white house at the end of the brick sidewalk. She hadn't wanted to come, but the others had out-voted her. "We should've told Ezra Menski we didn't want to come."

"But we *did* want to!" Chelsea pulled away from Roxie and looked at Kathy and Hannah with a look that said, "You agree with me, don't you?"

"That's right," they said.

"It's a great job for the *King's Kids.*" Chelsea flipped back her long red hair and looked smug. She was the president of *King's Kids* since she was the one who had thought up the idea of doing odd jobs to make money. When Roxie's grandma's new husband had asked all four of them to help clear out the personal property from Ezra's uncle's country home, Chelsea had been glad to accept. "It'll be fun to stay in the country in the big old house."

"Not to me." Shivering, Roxie glanced around for Grandma and Ezra. They'd been married over a month but still acted like honeymooners. It was disgusting. She finally spotted them outside the huge gray barn with a faded red roof. She started to call to them, but they stepped inside the barn, so she turned back to the Best Friends. "I'm sure not going in the house without Grandma!"

"Give me the key and I'll go in!" Laughing, Kathy tugged the house key out of Roxie's hand. "It'll be fun." She turned to Hannah and Chelsea. "Wanna come?"

"Sure." Chelsea giggled and headed for the door.

Hannah hung back. She didn't want to hurt Roxie's feelings. "Is it all right if we go in without you?"

Roxie shrugged. Just then Roxie glanced at an upstairs window—and saw someone looking out at her! A shadowy image stood behind the sheer curtain. Roxie shrieked and pointed but couldn't get out a word, she was so scared. By the time the girls looked to where she was pointing, the person was gone. "I saw . . . saw someone," she whispered hoarsely.

"Oh, sure." Chelsea giggled. "I know what

you're doing. Playing a trick on us to make us want to leave."

Helplessly Roxie shook her head.

"It won't work, Roxie." Kathy ran back toward the door. "Race you!"

Chelsea raced after Kathy and finally Hannah followed. They all wore jeans, sweatshirts, and sneakers. They were all ready to help Ezra and Roxie's Grandma Emma clean Lenny Menski's personal items out of the house.

Roxie frowned, looked up at the window again, shrugged, and walked up the curved sidewalk. She'd probably been mistaken. Sometimes her imagination played tricks on her. A shiver trickled down her spine. Why was she trying to fool herself? She *had* seen someone in the window! Why wouldn't the others believe her?

Kathy unlocked the door, then hesitated. The tiny blonde hairs on the back of her neck stood on end. What if Roxie really had seen someone inside? What if that someone was an insane escaped convict who leaped out at them and killed them right where they stood?

"What are you waiting for?" Chelsea reached around Roxie and pushed the door open. It squawked on its hinges, just like in that Frankenstein movie she'd watched late last Saturday night. The smell of furniture polish drifted out to them. Ezra had said no one had lived in the house since May, when his uncle went to visit his daughter in New Mexico. He'd stayed there a while, then decided not to return to Michigan at all. So he'd asked Ezra to take out his personal items and ship them to him. The furniture, appliances, and tools had been sold along with the house. The new owners wanted to move in November 15.

Roxie wrapped her arms around herself and rubbed her hands up and down the sleeves of her red sweatshirt. She didn't want to go inside, but she couldn't let the others walk into danger while she stayed outdoors. She heard them talking and laughing. Could she convince them she really had seen someone?

Slowly she stepped through the front door that led directly into the living room. A stone fireplace against the outside wall was flanked by a cherry wood gun cabinet lined with rifles and a shotgun on one side and a cherry wood very full bookcase on the other. A TV stood against a wall with a couch and love seat across from it. A cherry wood coffee table sat directly in front of the couch. Roxie frowned. She could almost see her reflection in the coffee table from the sunlight streaming in the windows. Nothing was dusty. No cobwebs hung in the corners. She backed up and bumped into a closet door. She hesitated, then peered inside. It was a walk-in closet with several coats hanging on a long bar. Above the coats on a shelf sat boxes of

Christmas decorations and several unmarked cardboard boxes.

Chelsea stuck her head through the doorway that led to the kitchen. "Roxie, this house is huge! Ezra said it's about a hundred and fifty years old, but it sure doesn't look it."

"I'd like to live here." Kathy peered out the kitchen window to the large shed several yards away. "Megan would love using that shed as a playhouse." Megan was Kathy's four-year-old sister, and she liked playing make-believe.

Hannah stood beside the long table in the dining room. Eight chairs sat around it. "It must've been terrible to live here alone like Lenny Menski did after his wife died."

Chelsea opened a door that led to a laundry room. She frowned. She could smell detergent and bleach as if it had just been used. She started to lift the white lid on the washer to see if it was wet inside, then laughed at her foolishness.

Finally Roxie followed the girls up the open staircase with shiny banisters. The steps creaked. The wide hall had four doors on each side—six giant bedrooms in all, and *three* bathrooms.

Hannah touched the lavender and blue bedspread in the master bedroom. "That's strange—it smells clean in here. Not as if the house had been shut for months."

Shivering, Roxie darted a look around. Maybe the person she'd seen kept the house clean.

"Ezra said someone comes regularly to air it out," Chelsea said as she looked in the closet. The aroma of apple and cinnamon drifted out. Several suits hung on one rod and shirts on another. Four pairs of shoes lined a wooden shoe rack. "Did Lenny Menski farm this place for a living?"

Roxie shrugged. Nothing about Grandma's husband or his family interested her. She looked out the window at the pasture and further on to the highway. She saw a truck and two cars but couldn't hear them.

"Look in here," Chelsea called from a room down the hall.

Roxie wanted to run down the stairs and outdoors, but she followed Hannah and Kathy. Her blue eyes wide, Chelsea stood in the end bedroom with a paper in her hand.

"What is it?" Hannah peered closer for a better look.

"Our last English assignment—to write a book report on *The Truth About Helen*." Chelsea bit her bottom lip. She'd heard a couple of girls talking about the book and giggling over the dirty language and the explicit sex scenes. Chelsea wanted to tell Mr. Borgman that she refused to read the book because she didn't feel it was right as a Christian to read it, but so far she hadn't found the courage.

Roxie jerked open the closet door. It was completely empty. She flushed. Had she expected to find someone hiding in there? "That paper proves it—I told you I saw someone in the window. And it was that very window!" She pointed to the window behind Hannah and Kathy. They jumped aside as if they'd been stung by a bee.

Kathy grabbed the paper from Chelsea. "I bet the woman who cleans the house left it by accident. She probably has a kid in sixth grade in Middle Lake."

"Probably." Hannah bit her lip. It did seem strange to find a sixth grade assignment sheet in Lenny Menski's house. She tapped the paper. "I told Mr. Borgman I won't read that book. I told him I'd read something else."

"What did he say?" Chelsea asked.

"That I'd get a failing mark." Hannah flipped back her long black hair. Her black eyes snapped. She had high cheekbones and a wide forehead. "I told him I still wouldn't read it."

Chelsea's stomach tightened. Could *she* be that brave? She didn't want to make a big deal of it, and she certainly didn't want a failing grade on it. But she would not read the book either.

Kathy shrugged. "My mom wrote Mr. Borgman a note and told him she won't let me read it. She said she'd rather have me get an E for the day than pollute my mind. He got really angry and gave me an E."

"That's not fair!" Chelsea's cheeks turned red, making her freckles blend together. "Why should we be forced to read a book like that?"

"Mr. Borgman says if we can't follow school policy, we should go to a Christian school." Her dark eyes snapping, Hannah leaned back against a desk. "It costs too much to send my sisters and me to a Christian school. And Mom says she really can't handle home schooling us, even though she'd like to."

Roxie frowned. "Lacy said in high school she has to refuse to read books assigned to her. They make her do twice as much work since she won't read the assigned books. But she won't give in."

"Good for her!" Kathy nodded, sending her short blonde curls bobbing. "Maybe we should send a petition around school for kids to sign who refuse to read the book."

Chelsea wrinkled her nose. "A lot of them would sign just because they don't want to read any book."

Kathy sighed. "I guess you're right. But we should think of something to do!"

Just then Roxie's grandma shouted to them from downstairs.

"We'll be right there," Roxie called back. Maybe *they'd* believe her if she told them about the shadowy image she'd seen in the window. But what if they didn't?

Chelsea folded the work sheet and pushed it into the pocket of her jeans as she hurried after Hannah.

Roxie stopped at the bottom of the stairs and looked back up. Was someone hiding up there? Roxie shivered.

2

The Noise in the Wall

Roxie stood to one side of the living room while the Best Friends clustered around Roxie's Grandma Emma and Ezra Menski.

"I left the groceries out in the car," Emma said. "Who wants to bring them in? The milk and eggs really should be in the refrigerator."

Hannah started for the door. "I'll get them."

Roxie's skin pricked with sudden fear. "You can't go alone! It's not safe!"

Ezra frowned, and his bushy brows almost met over his large beak-like nose. His pants and shirt hung loosely on his large frame. "What nonsense is that, Roxann?"

She flushed scarlet. Even if she told him, he'd never believe her. "None of us are used to being in the country," she finally said in a weak voice.

Hannah knew Roxie still didn't like Ezra even though he was her new grandpa. Hannah smiled and caught Kathy's arm. "Help me carry the groceries in, will you?"

"Sure." Kathy smiled at the others. She didn't want Roxie or Ezra to be upset. "We'll be right back."

Hannah ran to the station wagon with Kathy right behind her. A U-Haul trailer was hooked to the back of the station wagon. Hannah opened the back door of the station wagon and handed a bag of groceries to Kathy, then took the other in her arms. It had the milk and was heavier. "I wish Roxie would learn to like Ezra."

"She will. We've been praying, right?"

Hannah smiled and nodded. The Best Friends always prayed for each other.

Kathy walked slowly toward the house with Hannah at her side. "He is kind of gruff, but that's only his way."

"I know. I've told Roxie that." Hannah glanced at the upstairs windows. "I wonder what Roxie saw that made her think someone was up there."

"Probably a shadow of a dresser or even the way the curtains hang." Kathy shrugged and walked faster. Her pink sweatshirt suddenly felt too hot, even as a chill trickled down her spine.

Chelsea opened the door wide and let them in. They carried the bags to the kitchen and unloaded them.

"We sure won't go hungry these two days,"

Chelsea said as she put the milk and eggs in the refrigerator. She caught sight of a leaf of lettuce and frowned. It looked fresh. She shrugged. The cleaning lady had probably brought a sandwich with lettuce on it. It was no big deal. But she wouldn't mention it to Roxie just in case it frightened her. She knew Roxie sometimes got scared when she had no reason to.

Emma set to work making a pot of coffee. "I know you'll want coffee while you work, Ezra." She smiled lovingly at him, and he smiled back.

"You know me too well, Emma."

While the others talked and laughed together, Roxie slipped out of the kitchen and into the living room. She could remember the times Grandma had made coffee for Grandpa. She remembered the looks of love they'd exchanged. But now he lived in Heaven, and everybody said Grandma had every right to get married again. Roxie bit her lip. Why hadn't Grandma married someone nice?

Roxie perched on the edge of the couch with her chin in her hands and her elbows on her knees. If she were home right now, she'd be carving on the baby fox she'd started. The rest of her carvings were on display at Middle Lake Middle School in the case near the front doors. Anyone coming to school would see them and read the plaque with her name, age, and grade that Mrs. Evans, the principal, had had printed.

The aroma of freshly perked coffee drifted through the house. Roxie jumped up. She'd come here to work—not sit around and mope. She stuck her head in the kitchen. "I'll start carrying out the boxes in the closet in here."

"I'll help!" Smiling, Kathy hurried to Roxie.

"Leave the guns in the cabinet for me to pack," Ezra said gruffly.

Roxie bit back an impatient remark. She sure didn't want to pack the guns. She didn't know how to break one down even though Dad and Eli had showed her how with theirs.

"Chelsea and Hannah, you start upstairs in the closets," Emma said. "I'm sure you both want to get to work and not sit around and wait for us. Your young bones can take more action than ours can." Emma's brown eyes twinkled as she laughed. "You'll find packing boxes in the U-Haul."

"Grab a box from here on your way out," Roxie said from inside the walk-in closet near the front door. She handed each one a box, then lifted one down from the shelf for herself. Just then she heard a noise in the far wall of the closet. She froze, then relaxed. It was probably only a mouse. What else could be in the wall? She hurried after the others out into the bright sunlight.

Chelsea pulled a load of empty boxes out of the trailer. "I don't think it'll take us two days to do the job."

Hannah agreed. "But it'll be fun to stay in the country. We could go on a hike back in those woods." Most of the trees were bright red, orange, and yellow with a few tall, dark-green spruce trees with long sweeping boughs.

Just then a new red car with mud spattered on the sides pulled into the long driveway, and the girls turned to watch.

The sun glinted on the windshield, and they couldn't see who was driving. The tires crunched on the gravel drive.

"It could be a neighbor come to check us out," Kathy said. "We could be robbing the place for all they know."

"Or it could be a salesman." Roxie chuckled. "Mom should be here. She loves getting rid of salesmen!"

The car stopped beside the station wagon. Frowning, a man got out of the car. He was medium build and wore a gray suit, white shirt, and multi-colored tie. He brushed his short, brown hair back with his fingers.

Roxie moved closer to Hannah. There was something about the man that frightened her. She didn't speak, nor did the others. A crow was cawing like crazy out in the field.

The man slowly walked around his car and came up to them. Finally he smiled. Lines spread from the corners of his blue eyes into his hairline.

"Afternoon, girls. I'm looking for someone." He held out a school photo. "It's last year's picture, but she still looks like this. Do you know her?"

Chelsea shook her head.

"It's Bev Doanne," Roxie said.

Kathy nodded. "Sure, we know her."

Hannah agreed. "She's in sixth grade."

The man cleared his throat and brushed at his eyes. "It embarrasses me to say it, but she ran away from home, and I'm looking for her. I'm Jim Doanne, her dad. Have you seen her today?"

"There's no school today." Chelsea felt sorry for the man. She knew how her dad would feel if she ever left home.

Jim Doanne slipped the picture into his inside coat pocket. "Was she in school yesterday?"

Roxie shrugged as Hannah and Kathy said they hadn't noticed.

"If you see her, give me a call, will you?" Jim Doanne held a business card out, and Kathy finally took it. He looked toward the house. "You girls live here?"

"No." Roxie gave the girls a look to keep them from going into detail. "We're visiting."

"Mind if I look around?"

Roxie stiffened. "You'd have to ask Ezra Menski. He and my grandma are inside."

Jim Doanne narrowed his eyes. "Ezra Menski, you say."

"He's married to Roxie's grandma," Chelsea said before Roxie could stop her.

Abruptly Jim Doanne turned back to his car. "Let me know if you see Bev. Tell her I love her and want her back home where she belongs."

The girls stood close together and watched him drive away. When he reached the road Kathy said, "Bev doesn't seem the type to run away from home."

"I wonder why he came way out here to look for her. This is a long way to come." Hannah frowned thoughtfully. She loved solving mysteries, and this sure smelled like a mystery to her.

Kathy read the card. "They live in town at 2560 Grant Street. That's a nice part of town—big houses and yards. He's an attorney."

Hannah looked toward the house. "I wonder why he didn't want to talk to Ezra."

"I can understand," Roxie muttered.

"Let's ask Ezra if he knows Attorney Jim Doanne." Kathy ran toward the house, stopped, then ran back and picked up an empty packing box. She giggled. "We can't forget our job just because something really exciting might be happening."

Chelsea picked up a box and followed. "It's sad if she really ran away from home."

In the kitchen Roxie stood beside her grandma while the others told about Jim Doanne.

Ezra laughed and slapped his bony leg. "I know

why he wouldn't talk to me. I stopped him from talking mean to his wife. She's quiet and soft-spoken and he's not." Ezra leaned back in the kitchen chair. "I went to see my lawyer. It's in the same office complex with Jim Doanne. Doanne and his wife were standing in the hall, and he was yelling at her for not getting the car washed when he told her to. She was red with embarrassment, but she wouldn't speak up. So I did. 'You too lazy to get the car washed yourself?' I asked him. He slammed into his office without another word. She smiled at me and ran outdoors to the car."

Roxie's mouth almost dropped open in surprise. Ezra was big and gruff and mean, and yet he'd helped Mrs. Doanne. It was hard to picture him doing that.

"I'm glad you helped her." Emma reached over and squeezed Ezra's hand. "You have a big heart."

Hannah nudged Roxie as if to say, "I told you so." Roxie frowned, and Hannah dropped her arm to her side.

"I don't remember Bev," Chelsea said.

"She's not in our homeroom." Kathy laid the business card on the table. "She was in fifth grade last year. But she does have gym with us. She's kind of short and has long dark hair and brown eyes."

"She was the girl Kesha made fun of for being afraid to dive," Hannah said.

Chelsea thought a minute, then nodded. "I

remember. She wouldn't even put on her swimsuit that day."

Roxie frowned. "I've seen her dive. She's not a bit afraid."

"Very strange." Hannah's pulse leaped with excitement. This really was a mystery! When they got home again, she'd talk to Bev's friends and learn what she could. Her heart sank. When she got back home she'd have to face Mom again. But how could she tell Mom she'd broken the special pickle dish?

Emma pushed back her chair and stood up. She tugged her pink sweater down over her jeans. "Time to get to work. Girls, you do the closets throughout the house, and I'll start on the hutch and here in the kitchen."

"All the dishes stay except a flowered soup tureen." Ezra opened a cupboard door. "Lenny said he kept it on the top shelf where it wouldn't get used even when his family came to visit." Ezra looked on every top shelf. "That's strange."

Hannah jabbed Kathy and giggled. "A mystery."

"Oh, sure."

"Maybe it's in the buffet or the hutch." Emma hurried into the dining room and looked. "Did Lenny take it with him and forget he had?"

"He might be old, but he wouldn't forget a thing like that." Ezra looked through the cupboards again, this time on every shelf, even the very bottom ones. Finally he turned to the girls. "Keep your eyes open for it, will you? It's over a hundred years old and has been in the family since they came west from New York."

"Would the cleaning lady steal it?" Emma asked softly.

Ezra frowned. "She's very honest and reliable. But I'll give her a call to see if she saw it."

"A missing soup tureen and a missing girl." Hannah tapped her finger against her chin. "I wonder if there's a connection."

Chelsea tugged Hannah's hair. "How could there be?"

"You never can tell."

Roxie shook her head and walked to the closet to finish carrying out the boxes. There was only one left. Then she had to fold and pack the coats.

Kathy lifted a coat from its hanger and carefully folded it. "I'm sure glad my dad is nice and not like Bev's dad."

"Maybe he was just having a bad day."

"Maybe." Kathy dropped the coat into the box and reached for another one. "Have you ever met your dad's boss?"

Roxie giggled. "Is that a joke? My dad *is* the boss."

Kathy laughed. "I forgot."

"Did you meet your dad's boss?"

Kathy swallowed hard. "Sunday he and his family are coming to dinner."

"That's great!"

"But he's a famous TV preacher! I won't know how to act or what to say!"

"You won't have any problem, Kathy. I don't understand why you're so worried."

"Why do you say that?"

"Your dad's a famous TV musician, and you don't have any trouble talking to him."

"But he's my dad!"

"Ralph Gentry is somebody's dad too." Roxie tossed a coat over Kathy's head. "You're scared about nothing!"

Kathy flung the coat away, then giggled. "I guess you're right."

Just then Roxie heard the noise in the wall again. She gripped Kathy's arm and pointed at the wall. "Listen!"

Kathy listened but didn't hear anything. "Probably a mouse."

Roxie relaxed slightly. "I guess." But was it?

3

The Shed

Shivering even though the sun was still warm, Chelsea stopped just outside the shed and looked at the Best Friends. They were taking a break from working and had decided to go exploring. "I don't want to go in first! What if there's a mouse or something?"

"Or spiders." Making a face, Kathy stepped back from the shed. It was about the size of a two-car garage and stood between the house and the brightly colored woods. The shed had one door like a sliding barn door and two small windows that were surprisingly clean.

Hannah chuckled and stepped around Chelsea and Kathy. "I'll go in. It doesn't bother me." She slid the door open, and warm air rushed out at her along with the smell of gasoline. The biggest riding lawn mower Hannah had ever seen sat on one side of the shed near a wall covered with gardening tools hanging from a peg board. Several bushel baskets were piled in a corner. Cobwebs almost touched the lawn mower as they hung down from the rafters in all but one corner. Hannah frowned thoughtfully. It was as if someone had brushed away the cobwebs on one part of the shed. Slowly she walked to the corner and studied the area. She couldn't see any reason for it to be clean and the rest not.

"What do you see, Hannah?" Roxie crowded close to Hannah and looked around.

With a small squeal Chelsea jumped back out the door. "A mouse?"

Hannah shook her head. "I don't see anything. That's the whole point. See? Cobwebs all over except here."

Kathy backed away and almost tripped over a bucket. "That must mean someone's been in here."

Hannah nodded. "Who? Why? I think we need to find out."

Roxie impatiently shook her head. "What does it matter? Let's leave right now. I sure don't want to be in here if we're in danger."

Chelsea stepped farther away from the shed. A warm wind tousled her red hair. "Let's go back to the house."

Hannah crossed her arms and stayed put. "Are we a bunch of cowards? I don't think so. We have a mystery to solve, and I think we should solve it together."

"I don't." Roxie headed for the door.

Kathy looked from Roxie to Hannah. "There's nothing to be afraid of. So what if there are cobwebs missing? So what if someone cleaned them out? Nobody's here now." Kathy lifted her chin. "If we want to leave the shed, we should do it because we want to, not because we're scared into it."

Chelsea took a determined step forward, then another until she stood inside. "I agree! I say let's look around and see what we can see."

Roxie shivered, but she didn't leave the shed. She watched as the others looked around to find the reason for the clean area. "It's probably a simple reason. Something used to be there, and somebody moved it out."

"Who?" Hannah asked.

"The housekeeper, of course. She's the only one who's been here." Roxie shrugged. She could tell the idea sounded as ridiculous to the others as it did to her, but it was the only explanation.

Just then the unthinkable happened—a mouse streaked across the concrete floor. The girls screamed and ran out of the shed, then stopped several feet away under a big oak with fiery red leaves.

Hannah laughed helplessly. "I can't believe we ran away from a little scared mouse."

Chelsea sank to the grass. She waited until the others sat down with her. "Mice have always scared me. Once we went to see my granny—that's my great-grandma on my mom's side—near the Oklahoma/Arkansas border. She lived in a little run-down house in the country. I thought maybe she'd sit on a rocking chair on her porch with a hound dog beside her and a corncob pipe in her mouth." Chelsea giggled as she looked at the Best Friends. "Anyway, we were all eating breakfast one morning—at the table in the kitchen, not the porch—and two mice came out of hiding and sat right there eating some crumbs Mike had dropped. I started to scream, but Granny patted my shoulder and told me not to scare the mice away."

Roxie shivered and wrapped her arms around her legs. "I would've screamed anyway."

"They were kind of cute." Chelsea giggled. "They looked like the fat mouse in the *Cinderella* video."

"Clothes and all?" Kathy asked, then nudged Chelsea's arm and laughed. "I guess mice aren't as bad as rats."

"Rats! Yuk! Double yuk!" Roxie shivered. "Dad said at one of his construction sights he saw five rats! *Big* ones! He said they were so big and strong he put them to work laying bricks." Roxie fell over laughing as the others joined in.

Hannah's smile faded, and tears pricked her eyes. It felt good to laugh with friends. Before Chelsea had moved across the street from her a few months ago, she had never had friends to talk to or laugh with. Now she had three best friends! She'd prayed for a friend, and God had answered. Silently she thanked Him again right then. As long as she lived, she'd thank Him for her friends. He'd promised to give her more than she could even ask or think—and He had!

Kathy brushed an ant off her hand as she watched a thousand ants scurry around on their little hill. She looked closer. The ants were trying to pick up a piece of potato chip. "Somebody was here not long ago." She pointed to the chip. "It's not even soggy."

Shivers slithered down Roxie's spine, and she moved closer to Chelsea.

Hannah sucked in her breath. "I wonder if somebody's been trespassing. Whoever it was could've gone into the shed."

Roxie darted a frightened look around. "Where would he be now?"

Kathy jumped up and dramatically pointed up into the tree branches. "Up there, I bet! Ready to leap down on us!"

With a shriek Roxie scrambled up. "Do you see somebody?"

"She's only kidding," Chelsea said as she jumped up and brushed off her jeans. "Look how high the bottom branches are. You'd have to be a giant to reach them."

Roxie slumped in relief. She hated getting frightened, but lately *everything* scared her.

"I knew a giant once," Hannah said.

"The Jolly Green Giant from TV?" Kathy giggled.

Hannah shook her head. "He's seven feet tall! An Ottawa like me, and he plays basketball in college. He hates it when people tease him about being so tall."

"Like I hate being teased about my red hair and freckles." Chelsea flipped back her hair and rubbed a freckled hand across her freckled face.

Kathy twisted her toe in the grass. "I hate having people ask me if I'm going to be famous like my dad." She flung her arms wide and hunched her shoulders. "How do I know? I can't play any instrument, and I sure can't sing."

"Maybe you'll be an actress," Roxie shouted.

"Or a news reporter," Chelsea added.

Kathy shook her head. "I plan on being a cheerleader first before I think about things I'll do when I'm old. I don't even want to think about being famous someday."

Sighing, Roxie pushed the sleeves of her sweatshirt up to her elbows and looked toward the house. "Grandpa was a famous artist. I'll never forget him! I don't think Grandma even thinks about him any more. She's too busy with her new husband!"

Hannah touched Roxie's arm. "They're really

happy, Roxie. Your grandma isn't lonely any longer. And neither is Ezra."

"That's right," Kathy said.

Roxie didn't want to hear all the good points of Grandma and Ezra being together. "Let's go look in the barn before it gets dark out. Maybe we'll find kittens in there."

Hannah ran to the shed and started to close the door. Who had cleaned away the cobwebs and dropped the potato chip? Maybe it was a mystery she wouldn't have time to solve. She closed the door and ran to the barn with the Best Friends.

■

Inside the shed Bev Doanne crept from her hiding-place and watched the girls until they disappeared inside the barn. Bev swallowed hard and blinked back tears. She ran to the door to shout to the girls but stopped before she touched the door. Mom and Alexa would be very angry if she let anyone know where they were. Finally she turned, her heart feeling like a heavy chunk of ice. She took a deep breath and slowly let it out. "You can come out now. They're gone."

A portion of the shed wall slid open, and Bev's sister Alexa and her mom, Mallary Doanne, stepped out. They both looked frightened. Bev wanted to shout, "Just let me go back to Dad! I'm the one to blame!" But the words stayed locked inside her.

Mallary nervously brushed back her dark hair,

then rubbed her hands up and down her jeans. Her face was white with blue-black smudges under her eyes. "Who were they?" she whispered.

"Girls from Middle School." Bev gazed longingly out the window again. She wanted to ask them for help, but she knew Mom and Alexa were too frightened to speak to anyone. They were afraid Dad would find out where they were and force them to go home with him. Bev choked back a sob. Mom and Alexa would never go home until they were sure Dad would get professional help from a good counselor! They didn't know he lost control only because she kept making him so angry. If she were the daughter he really deserved, he would never beat any of them. If only . . .

Nobody but Grandma knew how he treated them. Grandma cleaned Lenny Menski's house, and she'd let them hide there until Mom could decide what to do. Grandma had showed them the secret room in the house behind the walk-in closet wall and the tunnel that led to the shed. It had been used as part of the "underground railroad" that helped runaway slaves get to freedom. Bev thought none of that was necessary, but Mom and Alexa did.

"What girls?" Alexa asked sharply. She didn't want any of her friends to know she was hiding out like a common criminal. And she'd never ever tell them her dad beat them!

Bev turned to her sister. A smudge of dirt ran

down the side of Alexa's face, and her dark hair needed brushing. "Roxie Shoulders was one of them. Her sister Lacy's in your class."

Alexa pressed her hands to her flushed cheeks. "It would be so embarrassing if she found us!"

"She won't! Nobody will!" Mallary wrapped her arms around herself and rocked back and forth. She'd started doing that lately—as if hugging herself would ease her pain. She shot a look at Bev. "Get away from the window before they see you."

Bev took a deep breath. She hadn't told her mom that Roxie had already seen her in the upstairs window. It would frighten her too much. "Mom, Roxie and Kathy Aber would help us. You remember them. Roxie's dad built our house, and Kathy's dad is on that religious TV program you watch."

Mallary nodded. "I remember those girls."

"Hannah Shigwam was with them too. And a new girl—Chelsea McCrea."

"I don't want anyone to know about us. I mean it!" Mallary trembled and leaned weakly against the wall. "It took us a long time to find the courage to walk away from your dad. We can't let him find us." Mallary's face blanched. "We've lived too long in fear."

Bev's face burned with shame. Why couldn't she blurt out the truth? Dad hated her and because he did, he got angry at them all!

Alexa ran over to her mom and put her arms around her. "We'll make it, Mom," she whispered.

Bev pushed her hair back with shaking hands. "The girls know how to pray, Mom. They'd help us. Let me tell them we're here."

"No! Promise you won't give us away, Beverly. Promise!"

Bev groaned and finally nodded.

"Where will we sleep tonight? Or eat?" Alexa helplessly shook her head. "I'm hungry."

Mallary slipped an arm around Alexa's slender shoulders. "Don't worry. We'll find a way to get blankets, and then we'll sleep right here in the shed or even in the hidden room behind the closet."

Bev ducked under a cobweb, then leaned against the wall. "Why didn't Grandma tell us they were coming?"

"Maybe she tried and couldn't." Alexa smiled weakly. "I bet she'll try to help us yet today. If it were safe, we could stay with her tonight."

Mallary shook her head hard. "Your dad watches her place."

Alexa swallowed the lump in her throat that she got every time she thought about Dad. "Why does Dad hate us so much?"

"He doesn't hate us!" Mallary had said it over and over, but Bev knew the truth. "He loves us. He just can't control his emotions. Grandma said a psychologist told her something really bad must've happened to him when he was a kid and he never got over it. He needs help to resolve it, and help to control his anger."

Alexa impatiently brushed a tear off her cheek. "I wish we had a dad like Lacy Shoulders's dad. He's always so nice!"

Bev walked to the window and looked out again. The girls stood outside the barn talking and laughing. Bev's heart turned over. How she wanted to run to them and beg for help!

Hot tears filled her eyes and ran down her cheeks.

4

Sue Monroe

Savoring the last bite of her chocolate cake with rich, gooey chocolate frosting, Kathy looked around the table as they sat talking after dinner. If only Sunday's dinner would be this easy! It was fun talking to Emma and Ezra Menski, but it sure wouldn't be fun to talk to Ralph Gentry and his family. Dad had said Ralph Gentry had thirteen-year-old twins—a boy and a girl. Duke and Brody were excited about meeting them. Kathy wadded her paper napkin. She wouldn't know what to say or how to act.

"You're awfully quiet, Kathy," Emma said as she set her empty coffee cup down. "Anything bothering you?"

Kathy shrugged. She couldn't tell them she was afraid for Sunday to come. They wouldn't understand why she was nervous about meeting Ralph Gentry and his family.

"I hope we didn't work you too hard today," Ezra said in his gruff voice. The skin on his face sagged, and he looked old and tired.

"Tomorrow we'll have a picnic in the woods if the weather is as nice as today." Emma smiled at the girls. She looked as fresh and full of energy as she had when they'd started working this morning.

Roxie thought about the wild animals in the woods and shivered. She didn't want a squirrel to jump off a limb and land on her shoulder. Or what if they startled a deer and it ran right over her? Or what if a fox bit her on the ankle?

"A picnic would be fun," Hannah said with a nod. Staying busy with work or play helped keep her mind off the pickle dish tragedy. She saw Roxie's frown and wished she'd kept quiet. She didn't want to do anything that would make the girls drop her as a friend.

Her eyes wide, Chelsea wadded her napkin in her lap. "Are there bears out there?"

The others laughed, and Chelsea relaxed. Someone had told her bears still lived in Michigan.

"You might find a bear way up north, but not around here," Ezra said as he pushed back his chair.

Just then someone rang the front doorbell. Kathy jumped up. "I'll get it." The smell of coffee followed her as she hurried through the hall to the living room. The closet door stood open, so she closed it, then opened the front door. A woman older than Kathy's mom but younger than Emma stood there with a huge purse that looked heavy over her arm. She wore dark slacks, a red blouse, and a red and navy jacket. She had dark eyes and dark hair with a few streaks of gray. She smiled, but her eyes were full of worry. She glanced past Kathy, then back at her.

A tiny shiver trickled down Kathy's spine. "Can I help you?"

"I'm Sue Monroe. I clean the house for Lenny Menski."

Kathy smiled in relief. There was nothing to worry about. "Ezra Menski mentioned you. Come in. He's at the dinner table."

"Oh, I hope I didn't stop in at a bad time."

"It's all right. We're done."

"Please tell him I'm here." Sue Monroe moved from one foot to the other.

"Just go on into the kitchen."

"Oh, I don't want to intrude."

Kathy hesitated, then hurried to the kitchen.

Her heart hammering, Sue Monroe ducked into the closet, turned a very small hook on the wall, and watched the back section of the closet twist to reveal a small dark room. "Mallary," Sue whispered, "I brought food." She set down the huge purse, then quickly closed the door and stepped out of the closet.

Ezra was standing there with the Best Friends

and Emma. They all looked at Sue Monroe questioningly.

Hannah narrowed her eyes. Why was the woman acting so nervous? Had she stolen or broken the valuable soup tureen and later realized that Ezra would notice it was missing, so she'd come to admit what she'd done?

Sue flushed at being caught in the closet. "I left something in the hall closet, and I wanted to get it."

"But we already took everything out of there." Roxie locked her hands behind her back. "We thought it was all Lenny Menski's. Did we pack something of yours?"

Sue fingered the collar of her red blouse. "I left a coat here last week when it was cold."

"We packed all the coats." Kathy tried to remember the coats from the closet but couldn't.

Emma stepped forward with a smile. "We marked all the packing boxes, so we'll be able to find the box from the front closet without too much trouble."

"Thank you! It's a dark blue, calf-length coat."

Roxie shook her head. "It wasn't there. All of them were either gray or black."

Emma patted Roxie's back. "Dark blue and black look much the same if the room is dark. We'd better check the box." She started for the door.

"Wait!" Sue laughed nervously. "How silly of

me! I just remembered—I took it home the other day."

Hannah smelled a mystery but didn't know what to do about it. Every nerve tightened, and she wanted to leap into immediate action, but she knew she'd have to wait for more evidence.

Just then Kathy realized that Sue Monroe was no longer carrying her purse. She started to speak just as Ezra did, so she held back her question. She glanced around but couldn't see the purse anywhere. How strange!

"I'm glad you stopped in." Ezra wrapped his bony fingers around his wide suspenders. "Lenny wanted me to give you a box of things he thought you'd like."

Sue Monroe's eyes filled with tears, and she quickly brushed them away. "How kind of him! But it's not at all necessary." She cleared her throat. "I should be going."

"What about your purse?" Kathy asked, her own voice sounding loud in her ears.

With a shaky laugh, Sue shook her head and spread her hands. "How silly of me. I left it in the closet when I went in there. I'll get it." She quickly opened the closet and stepped inside, hoping Mallary had had a chance to unload it and set it back out. Sure enough, it sat on the floor. In great relief she picked it up and walked back to the others.

Kathy studied the purse. It looked different—

why, it was practically empty. It didn't seem to hang as heavily on Sue Monroe's arm as it had just moments earlier. Kathy hid a grin. How ridiculous! She was getting as bad as Hannah when it came to imagining a mystery at every turn.

"Wait a minute and I'll get the box Lenny packed for you." Ezra picked up a box from inside the living room and carried it to Sue. "Here are a few collectibles Lenny wanted you to have. I'll carry it for you."

Hannah took a step forward. "I'll carry it, Ezra. You go have another cup of coffee and a piece of chocolate cake."

Ezra smiled as he handed the box to Hannah. "Why, thank you. I'll do just that."

The Best Friends looked at Hannah to see what she was up to. They knew she was sniffing out a mystery, though Ezra didn't.

"We'll go with you, Hannah," Kathy said quickly. Maybe it wasn't her imagination after all.

Chelsea opened the door. A warm breeze brought in the smell of pine. A horn honked in the distance.

Roxie nervously chewed her bottom lip and waited until the others walked out, then finally followed. What was Hannah thinking? There wasn't anything wrong with Sue Monroe. Or was there?

At Sue's car the Best Friends stood patiently while Sue opened the trunk. Hannah carefully set the box next to a folded blanket. The smell of tuna drifted out.

Hannah turned to Sue. "We've been looking for a blue flowered soup tureen that Lenny Menski especially wants. Have you seen it?"

Sue nodded. "Sure, I've seen it. It's on the top shelf above the refrigerator."

"Ezra looked, and it's not there," Roxie said.

Sue stiffened. "That's strange. It was there last week."

"Who could've taken it?"

Sue glanced around. She knew Mallary and the girls wouldn't take anything. "I don't know!" She frowned in thought. "There was a man here a couple of weeks ago who wanted to buy antiques. But I wouldn't let him in the house. I don't think he could get in to steal anything."

"I wonder if other things are missing that we don't even know about," Hannah said.

"I think Lenny keeps a list of his collectibles and antiques in the desk drawer in his bedroom. Tell Ezra to check it out." Sue glanced in the box, then gasped. She lifted out an old apple peeler. "I can't believe he wanted me to have this! It's very old and was a special treasure to him."

"Ezra said Lenny had put the box of things together before he left, then put them on a shelf in the laundry room," Roxie said.

Sue moved aside a few things, then lifted a

newspaper up. Under it was the blue flowered soup tureen. "Look! Ezra must've given me the wrong box. I'll take it right back inside. We'll have to call Lenny and get this straightened out."

The Best Friends looked at each other, followed Sue back inside the house, then listened as she explained to Ezra about finding the soup tureen.

"I'm sure he didn't want me to have the apple peeler," Sue said as she held it up. "He always treasured it because he used it when he was a boy at his grandma's."

"How strange." Ezra stroked his chin in thought. "I'll give Lenny a call right now."

Barely able to contain their excitement, the Best Friends helped Emma clear the table and load the dishwasher while Ezra made the call. Finally he hung up, and they all stood silently, watching him.

"Lenny said he gave you a sugar bowl and creamer, a cranberry red pitcher with matching vases, a copy of *Uncle Tom's Cabin*, and an etched glass bud vase."

Sue dabbed her eyes, then cleared her throat. "He knew I especially liked those things. Would they be in a different box in the laundry room?"

Ezra shook his head. "We took out everything." He touched the box on the counter. "This is the only box with antiques and collectibles in it."

Hannah's eyes flashed with excitement. This was a real mystery! She looked at the Best Friends with an unspoken question—would they help her solve it? They each nodded, though Roxie was the last to agree.

Emma looked through the box. She held up a silver dollar. "It's dated 1799," she said in awe.

Ezra took the coin and studied it, then shook his head. "He kept this put away for as long as I can remember. Who would know where to look for it?"

"I've never seen it before," Sue said quickly. "You must understand, I'd never steal anything!"

"Of course not." Ezra narrowed his eyes. "Who else came in here?"

Sue flushed hotly. She couldn't tell him about Mallary and the girls—she just couldn't! "I guess only the man I said wanted to buy antiques. But he was only at the front door—and not for very long."

"What was his name?" Hannah asked.

Sue frowned as she tried to remember. Her mind had been so full of her daughter and grand-daughters for such a long time that she sometimes forgot other things. "I'm not sure. I think it started with a G—maybe Galley or something like that."

Hannah pulled the phone book from the drawer and laid it on the counter. She opened it to the Yellow Pages while Ezra and Emma walked Sue to the door.

Chelsea looked over Hannah's shoulder and down at the Yellow Pages. "Did you find anything?"

"Not yet."

Roxie swallowed hard and forced back a shiver. "How would the man get in here?" She also thought but didn't say, *What if he's hiding in the house right now, just waiting to make trouble for us?*

Kathy locked her fingers together and took a deep breath. "I have something to tell you before Ezra and Emma get back," she whispered. She waited until they were looking at her in anticipation. In a hushed voice she told them how Sue's big purse had suddenly gotten lighter. "I don't know how it could happen. And maybe I'm imagining things."

"Unless she unloaded something while you were getting Ezra." Thoughtfully Hannah tapped her lips with her finger. This was more exciting than anything that had happened so far! "But what—and where?"

Chelsea headed for the closet. "Let's take a look."

Shivering, Roxie hung back, then ran after the Best Friends. She didn't want to be by herself for even a second. She stood in the closet with them and looked all around. What were they searching for anyway? The ceiling light cast a glow onto the shelves and onto the floor. The closet was totally empty. They didn't notice the special hook because it was so small and placed in the shadows.

Disappointed, Hannah leaned back against the wall. She caught the faint aroma of tuna but couldn't quite recognize the smell. "I guess I was wrong. She didn't leave anything in here."

"She didn't have time to go anywhere else." Chelsea tapped on the wall. "Wouldn't it be funny if there was a secret passage in here just like in that movie we saw?"

"Maybe Ezra knows." Hannah's dark eyes lit up. "Let's ask him."

Chelsea giggled. "I was only joking."

Roxie moved closer to Kathy. What if there *was* a secret passage or some secret rooms? Someone, *anyone*, could be hiding, just waiting to leap out at them and hurt them. What if . . .

5

The Sleepover

We forgot to finish looking in the Yellow Pages," Hannah said, heading out of the closet and back to the kitchen. Her steps were quiet on the carpeted floor.

Kathy peered out the window beside the front door. It was already getting dark outside. She could see flashes of headlights from the highway. With their arms around each other, Ezra and Emma were standing near the station wagon talking. Sue Monroe's car was gone. Kathy hurried to the kitchen with the others.

"There aren't many antique dealers around here," Chelsea said as they all stood at the counter and studied the Yellow Pages. "But maybe the man was from Grand Rapids. Or Battle Creek."

"Or Kalamazoo," Roxie added.

Hannah sighed heavily. Finding the needed information wouldn't be as easy as they'd hoped.

"Here's one that starts with G—Godfrey. But that doesn't sound a bit like Galley."

"How about this one?" Roxie pointed to the name Marvin Deck. "A galley is a kitchen on a boat, and a boat also has a deck."

Hannah shrugged. "Could be. We could call and see."

Kathy leaned against the counter and crossed her arms. "What would we say? 'Did you put a bunch of antiques in a box in Lenny Menski's house? Do you plan to steal them?' What?"

"I don't know," Hannah said with her head bent and her glossy black hair covering her cheek.

Chelsea looked at her watch. "It's too late now anyway. He'd be closed for the night."

Roxie rubbed her icy hands up and down her arms trying to warm herself. Could she handle spending the night here? Maybe she should call and ask Dad to pick her up. He'd do it. Or maybe Ezra would drive her back to town. She shook her head slightly. No way would she ask Ezra to do anything for her!

Just then Ezra and Emma walked in hand in hand. They brought a smell of fresh, cool autumn air with them. "It's turning a little chilly tonight," Ezra said. "I'll start a fire in the fireplace."

"We could roast marshmallows." Chelsea looked into the bag of food they'd brought. The bag crinkled. "Do we have any?"

Emma nodded and chuckled. "You know me. I came prepared for everything. I love toasted marshmallows too."

Chelsea dug deeper into the bag. "They're not in here."

"Did anyone put them in a cupboard?" Emma opened cupboards as she talked. "Or the refrigerator?"

The Best Friends looked at each other with wide eyes. They hadn't touched the marshmallows, and yet the treats were gone. Where had they disappeared to?

"Maybe you forgot to bring them," Ezra said as he poured himself another cup of coffee. Steam rose from his cup, sending the aroma through the kitchen.

Looking puzzled, Emma shook her head. "I know I brought them. Girls, are you playing a trick on me?"

"No," they all said at once.

"This is very strange." Emma looked quickly through the cupboards again, then the refrigerator, then the bag. "I can't understand this at all!"

"Another mystery," Hannah said brightly.

Roxie trembled. She didn't like the idea of facing anything else that could mean danger or trouble.

Ezra set his cup down and wrapped his hands around his wide suspenders. "There has to be a logical explanation. While we're trying to find it, let's go to the living room and get that fire going." He pulled Emma to his side and walked out with her.

"This is very strange," Hannah whispered.

Kathy shivered. "Is it even safe to stay here?"

Roxie's mouth turned as dry as an overbaked cake. If Kathy thought it wasn't safe, then it must not be! Roxie's stomach knotted. Why hadn't she stayed home where she belonged?

"It's safe." Chelsea giggled and tugged on the bottom of Kathy's shirt. "You're sure being silly, Kathy Aber. Nobody's in here but us."

"We didn't ask about the secret passage or hidden room. Let's do it now!" Hannah rushed to the living room, and the others followed close behind.

Ezra knelt by the fireplace and watched the fire kindle. Emma sat in the rocker watching him. The smell of burning wood filled the room. Flames crackled and licked at the wood.

Hannah stopped near Ezra. Electricity seemed to travel over her body and up and down her long black hair. "Ezra, could there . . . could there be a secret passage or hidden room in this house?"

He slowly stood up, and the bones in his knees cracked. "There sure enough is!"

The Best Friends gasped and stared in shock at each other, then back at Ezra.

"I'd forgotten all about it!" he exclaimed.

Hannah clasped her hands together. "Where is it?"

Roxie sank weakly to the couch. She didn't know if she wanted to hear this.

Kathy and Chelsea stepped closer to Hannah.

Ezra ran a bony hand over his balding head. "Lenny never would tell me. He said he wanted to keep the secret."

"But what if someone knows about it and is hiding there?" Hannah asked excitedly.

Roxie turned white and bit back a moan.

Kathy shivered.

Chelsea peered intently at Ezra to see if he was joking about the hidden room. He didn't seem to be.

"That's very unlikely," Emma said. "Ezra, don't frighten the girls."

"I didn't mean to." Ezra sank to a chair and rested his hands on the arms of it. "Lenny said this place was used to get slaves to freedom. He said he liked knowing about the secret passage and that I was free to try to find it. I gave up looking a long time ago."

"Call him and ask him to tell you where the secret room is," Hannah said. "Something mysterious is going on, and we need to see if someone is hiding in it."

"Call him, Ezra," Emma said softly. "I'd feel better myself."

Ezra spread his hands wide and shook his head. "He said he was just leaving for the weekend, and he didn't say where he was going."

"Would his daughter know?"

"They were all going."

Tingling with excitement, Hannah perched on the edge of the couch between Roxie and Kathy, who were both *very* tense. Forcing down panic, Chelsea sat on the floor with her back almost touching Kathy's legs.

"Who else knows where the hidden room is?" Emma asked.

"Nobody that I know of." Ezra rubbed his jaw. "I could call some of the family, but I don't think it would do any good."

"Let's go home," Roxie said hoarsely.

Ezra scowled at her. "No need to. We're safe here."

A log snapped in the fireplace and everyone jumped, then laughed uneasily.

"I think it's time to read the 91st Psalm." Emma leaned forward and smiled at everyone. "Roxann, please hand me my purse."

Roxie hurried across the room where the black leather purse sat on top of a box. She carried the purse to her grandma, then sat back down.

Emma pulled out a small Bible and in a clear, pleasant voice read the promises of protection in the 91st Psalm. The verses about "resting in the shadow of the Almighty" and God covering them with His wings and sending His angels to watch over them so "no harm will befall you" were comforting words for that scary evening. Chelsea, Hannah, and Kathy relaxed as they listened, thankful to know God was indeed taking care of them.

Roxie locked her icy hands together and tried to listen, but the words her grandma read seemed to drift over her head and dissolve in mid-air. Roxie heard the creak of the house, the snap of the wood in the fireplace, and a million criminals breathing in a secret passage behind the couch. *Does* every *room have a secret passage or hidden room?* she wondered. What if someone walked in and slit her throat while she was sleeping that night? Icicles splintered inside her chest, turning her blood cold.

Later while Ezra and Emma sat in front of the fireplace the Best Friends slowly walked upstairs to go to bed. Chelsea and Hannah would be sharing one room and Kathy and Roxie another.

Frowning, Chelsea pulled the work sheet from her pocket. "We forgot to ask Sue Monroe about this! I forgot I even had it."

Roxie swallowed hard. "I think we should all sleep in the same room. Like a . . . a sleepover!" She tried to sound excited instead of frightened. She didn't think she'd succeeded.

"Let's do it," Kathy said, nodding her blonde head. The idea of staying together made her feel better too.

"We can make plans." Hannah unfolded a

blanket and spread it at their feet. "I say we sleep on the floor since the bed is too small for all of us."

"I agree." Chelsea pushed the paper back into her pocket and picked up a pillow and blanket. "This will be fun." She dug her toothpaste and toothbrush out of her bag and led the way to the bathroom.

Later they lay in the dark with moonlight shining through the window—the very window where Roxie had seen the shadowy image. None of them wanted to remember that, but they all did, especially Roxie.

"Maybe we can find the hidden room and secret passage tomorrow," Hannah said softly.

Roxie wrapped herself tighter in her blanket. "It's so scary!"

"I think it's exciting!" Chelsea flipped onto her stomach. "I'd like a secret passage from my bedroom at home to someplace outdoors. I could go in and out and nobody would even know."

Roxie sat up with her blanket around her shoulders. "Once when I was ten I snuck out of the house at night and went to my friend Addie's house to stay." Roxie giggled softly, then sighed. She'd be afraid to try it now. "I walked by myself almost a block. Addie was waiting for me. We giggled and talked in her room until 3 in the morning, then finally fell asleep. It was summertime, so we didn't have school the next day."

"What happened when your folks found out?" Hannah asked. She knew she'd have been spanked hard if she ever did such a thing.

Roxie wrinkled her nose. "I was grounded for a whole entire week!"

"I'd still be grounded if I ever did that." Kathy slowly sat up. "Sometimes I think my mom and dad are too strict. They say it's because they love me. But I sure do wonder."

"They love you," Chelsea said in her Oklahoma accent. "I can tell by the way they talk to you and look at you."

Hannah flipped back her hair. "My dad says parents who really love their kids make them obey and don't spoil them. I think of that when they punish me." She thought of the pickle dish, and her mouth turned as dry as the dust balls under the bed. "Sometimes I wonder if parents could stop loving their kids because of bad things they do." *Like not telling them you did something and letting your twin sisters take the blame*, she thought to herself, but she didn't say it.

Chelsea rested her chin on her knees. "I thought my dad quit loving me when he made us move from Oklahoma here to Michigan. But he didn't. I know that now. And I thought he didn't love me when he made me pay my own phone bill, but he loved me. I don't think we could do *anything* to make them stop loving us."

Kathy ran her hand up and down the soft blanket. "They might hate me if I do something stupid Sunday when Dad's boss comes to dinner."

"You won't do anything stupid," Hannah said softly.

"I might."

"Like what?" Chelsea jabbed Kathy's arm. "Spill soup on him?"

The girls laughed. Then Hannah said, "Soup . . . That reminds me of the blue flowered soup tureen. How did it get into the box in the laundry room? Was someone planning to steal it?"

"Somebody already stole Sue Monroe's box," Roxie said with a shudder. "Who? When?" Her voice rose, and she clamped her mouth closed so she wouldn't start screaming.

"We'll find out," Hannah said firmly. "And we'll start first thing in the morning."

Chelsea yawned. "I'm too tired to talk any longer. Now, that's tired." She settled down on her pillow and closed her eyes. "I'm sure glad we have angels watching over us. We can sleep without being afraid."

Roxie pictured angels guarding them, and she slowly stretched out and closed her eyes. Angels were watching over them! Silently she thanked God for them.

"Good night," Kathy said softly as she turned on her side.

"Sleep tight." Hannah giggled. "Don't let the bedbugs bite. My grandma always says that to me."

"I wonder whose work sheet that is." Chelsea's eyes popped open. "I'd sure like to know."

Hannah lifted her head slightly. "Wouldn't it be funny if it belonged to Bev Doanne?"

"Real funny," Kathy said dryly.

"If Bev's paper is here, is Bev too?" Roxie whispered.

The Best Friends gasped, then laughed. Bev was probably safely home by now, right where she belonged.

■

In the hidden room behind the closet Bev Doanne shivered and moved closer to Alexa. Her stomach ached from eating too many marshmallows from the bag she'd taken from the kitchen while everyone was outdoors. "I'm cold, Mom," Bev whispered.

"It's not safe yet to get another blanket. We'll wait until we're sure everyone is asleep." Mallary sounded tired and discouraged.

"I wish we'd stored blankets in here." Alexa moved restlessly.

"I do too," Mallary said. "But we didn't."

Bev's eyes stung with tears. She wanted to be home in her own bed. She wanted them to be a happy family. She turned her head away from Alexa and wiped her eyes with the back of her hand. The smell of tuna hung in the room. Grandma had brought them tuna sandwiches, cans of apple juice, and a bag of potato chips, plus homemade chocolate-chip cookies. Bev poked her stomach. If she were home, she'd have a bowl of cornflakes with a sliced banana on top. If she were home, she'd tell Dad she'd be a perfect daughter from now on.

If she were home . . .

6

The Night Search

Roxie sat up with a start. She'd definitely heard a strange sound. Blood roared in her ears, and she couldn't even hear Kathy snoring. When Kathy laid on her back, she snored louder than Brody and Duke put together—or so Roxie had heard.

Right now Roxie's skin pricked with a million needles of fear. The moonlight showed the girls sleeping around her. Had it been Kathy's snores that had awakened her? Oh, how she wished it was! But she knew it had been something—or *someone*—else. Was someone sneaking around the house and bumping into things? Slowly Roxie stood, her blanket in a warm heap at her bare feet. Could she find the courage to peek out the bedroom door? She licked her dry lips.

Slowly, step by step, she walked toward the door. Kathy's snores got louder, and Roxie's heart felt like it would jump right out of her body, but she didn't stop moving until she touched the doorknob. It felt cold under her hand. She turned it ever so slowly. With a slight click the door opened. The air in the hall felt cooler and smelled fresher. "Jesus, thank You for always being with me," she whispered under her breath.

She stuck her head out the door and looked up and down the hall. Nobody was in sight. She held her breath and tried to hear every sound in the house. A floorboard creaked—but it sounded like a gunshot to Roxie. She jumped, closed the door, and leaned against it, breathing hard.

"Where are you going, Roxie?" Hannah whispered as she sat up.

Roxie swallowed hard. "Uh . . . nowhere."

"To the bathroom? Want me to go with you?"

"No."

Hannah picked up her flashlight, then crept over Kathy to Roxie. "What's wrong?"

Roxie shuddered. She was glad Hannah had awakened; now she could tell someone . . . "I heard something . . . Like somebody walking . . . or something."

Her pulse leaping with excitement, Hannah reached for the doorknob. "Let's check it out."

Roxie caught her bare arm. "What if someone is out there and tries to hurt us?"

"We'll be careful." Hannah carefully opened the door and peeked out. She smelled the cool air and heard a creak that could've been the normal sound a house makes at night or could've been someone walking around. She flashed her light but didn't see anything out of the ordinary. Ezra's and Emma's bedroom door was closed. Hannah looked over her shoulder at Roxie. "Coming?"

Roxie groaned. She didn't want to go, but she couldn't let Hannah go alone. Barely nodding, she walked out into the chilly hall behind Hannah. "Turn off the light," Roxie whispered. "If somebody is out there, he'll see it."

Hannah clicked off the light but held it firmly in her hand. She used her free hand to grip the banister as she walked stealthily down the stairs. She stopped in the middle of the living room. Moonlight shone through the windows so brightly that she didn't need her flashlight. She looked toward the kitchen door, then over at the walk-in closet. The door was wide open. A chill raced down her spine, and she was thankful Roxie was right beside her. She nudged Roxie and pointed at the closet door, then pushed her mouth against Roxie's ear and whispered, "It's open."

Roxie's muscles bunched, ready to spring up the stairs if someone suddenly appeared.

Hannah crept to the closet door and peered inside. It was empty as far as she could see. She flashed her light inside to check it out, and it was indeed empty. She silently closed the door, careful not to let the click sound loudly. "Let's look in the kitchen."

Roxie frantically shook her head.

Hannah caught the sleeve of Roxie's pajamas and tugged her across the room. They stopped just inside the kitchen. Hannah looked around, while Roxie closed her eyes tight. Just then they heard a click from the laundry room, then felt a blast of cold air, then heard another click. Roxie grabbed Hannah's hand with both of hers and held on tight.

Hannah tried to speak but couldn't. Her legs felt weak, but she forced herself to walk to the laundry room. No one was there, but someone had definitely just opened the back door and closed it. She carefully moved aside the curtain and looked out the window. The moonlight showed the side yard and a part of the driveway. Nothing was moving out there. A cloud slid over the moon and left the yard in total darkness. Shaking her head, Hannah dropped the curtain back in place.

"Let's go back to our room," Roxie whispered hoarsely as she tugged on Hannah's hand.

Reluctantly Hannah walked back into the kitchen. She clicked on the flashlight to keep from tripping on the table and chairs. She looked over her shoulder into the laundry room, then flashed the light in there. The cupboard door above the washer was open! Hannah gasped. "Look!" she whispered, touching the cupboard door with the beam of light.

Roxie whimpered and bit back a scream of terror.

Hannah hurried to the laundry room and flashed the light on the shelves inside. They were as empty as when they'd unloaded them. Slowly she closed the door. If they'd left the box with the soup tureen and other special items inside, would it be gone now? Had someone come to steal that very box?

Roxie took a deep breath and slowly let it out. "Somebody was in here, right?"

"I think so."

"Please, let's go back upstairs!"

"I guess we'd better." Hannah led the way to the living room. She flashed the light over the fireplace and onto the empty gun cabinet, the TV, and the few boxes Ezra hadn't loaded yet.

"Come on!" Roxie jerked Hannah's hand.

Reluctantly Hannah walked upstairs with Roxie.

■

Behind the boxes in the living room Bev wiped cold sweat from her face, then slowly stood, clutching a blanket against her chest that she'd taken off the empty bed upstairs. What if the two girls had caught her? Maybe it would've been better. Maybe she should run upstairs and talk to them. But why even think about it? She couldn't do it. Her mother wouldn't let her.

She stood quietly until her heartbeat returned to normal, then started for the closet. She stopped. Moonlight once again streamed across the floor, making a path on the carpet. Now was her chance to call Dad. She'd started to a few minutes earlier, but someone had slid a key into the back door, so she'd dashed to the living room to hide behind the boxes. She'd heard someone moving around in the kitchen, then heard someone walking down the steps. Whoever had come in the back door slipped out when he heard the girls.

Bev dropped the blanket beside the closet door and tiptoed to the kitchen to use the phone. Her hand trembled as she picked up the receiver and punched the numbers. Dad answered on the first ring as if he'd been sitting right next to the phone. Had he answered the phone in his study, his bedroom, the kitchen, or was he watching TV in the living room with the cordless phone beside him as he often did?

Bev licked her dry lips. "Dad . . . It's me." It was hard to talk around the lump in her throat.

"Bev! Where are you?"

"With Mom and Alexa."

"Are you okay?"

"Yes."

"Where are you? I'll come get you."

She gripped the receiver so tightly her hand hurt. "I . . . I can't tell you."

He was quiet a long time. "Please come home!"

"I want to," she whispered.

"Get your mom on the phone."

Bev swallowed hard. "I can't."

"Come home, Bev. I miss you. I miss Mom and Alexa. Will you tell them?"

Bev took a deep breath. She had to tell him what she'd rehearsed over and over in her head until it had become like a school recitation. She sank to the floor and huddled against the counter to keep her voice from carrying to the others in the house. "Daddy, I promise to be a good daughter."

"You already are."

"No, not good enough. Or you wouldn't . . . get so mad at me. Or at Mom and Alexa."

"I just want all of you home!"

"I'll do everything just right. I mean it. I won't ever have my friends over when you don't want them there."

"Get your mom on the phone right now, Beverly!"

Tears ran down her cheeks. "I'll study hard and get all As."

"Shut up and get your mom!"

"I won't ever burn the toast again."

"Stop it!"

But she couldn't. She had to say it all just as she'd said it inside her head. "And I'll be real quiet when you're watching TV."

"Get home *now*!"

"I'll be perfect so you'll love me."

"I *do* love you," he snapped.

"Really, Daddy?" Bev sat up straight and wiped at her tears with her free hand.

"Get yourself home right now!"

"I can't. Mom and Alexa won't let me."

"Tell me where you are and I'll come get you."

Bev shook her head. "I want to tell you. Honest, I do. But I promised Mom I wouldn't. She said you have to stop hitting us before we'll come home."

"I'll stop. I promise!"

Bev bit her lip. She'd heard him say that for years, but he never kept his word. Would he this time because of the promises *she'd* made?

"Bev . . . Bev, honey, listen to me . . . I'll change. I mean it. I won't hit any of you ever again, no matter what you do to make me angry. Just come home! Please."

Bev's pulse leaped. He sounded as if he really meant what he said this time. She pushed her tangled hair back. "I have to go. I'll call you tomorrow."

"Don't hang up!"

"I have to. Mom's probably already worried about me."

"Are you at your grandma's?"

"No." Bev gasped. She wasn't supposed to tell

him that. "I got to hang up. Bye, Dad. Don't worry about us. We're all right."

"Does your grandma know where you are?"

"I'm not saying."

"She does know! The witch!"

"Don't hurt her! I didn't say she knows!"

"Tell me where you are and I promise not to hurt her."

Bev whimpered. He'd never hit Grandma before. Would he now if she didn't tell him?

"Tell me!"

"I . . . I can't . . . I just can't!"

He was quiet a long time. "I love you, Bev." His voice broke. "Tell your mom and Alexa I love them."

"I will." Bev hung up before she blurted out where she was. Was he really crying the way it sounded, or was it an act like in the past? She brushed at her tears. Should she call him back and tell him where they were? She touched the phone, then jerked her hand back. She had promised her mom she wouldn't.

Slowly Bev walked back to the living room, picked up the blanket, and stepped into the closet. Before tonight they'd slept upstairs, snug and warm in the beds. But now . . .

■

Upstairs Hannah lay with her eyes wide open, watching the moonlight. "Roxie, are you still awake?"

70

"Yes. I can't sleep."

"Maybe we should wake up Ezra and tell him someone was here."

"I guess so." But Roxie didn't want to do that. She didn't want to step one foot out of the room until daylight.

Hannah didn't move. "But what if we're wrong? I'd hate to wake him and your grandma if it was just our imagination."

"Me too." Roxie bit her lip and brushed at her eyes. How she hated to be so frightened! "Hannah, do we really have angels watching over us?"

"Sure we do. The Bible says so, and we know God's Word is true."

"Sometimes I forget."

"You have to remind yourself of the promises in the Bible. Read them over and over. Say them out loud. Then you won't forget. When you start getting scared, you can thank God that He's always with you to take care of you and that He sends angels to protect you, just like your grandma read tonight."

"I wonder if Bev Doanne knows she has angels watching over her."

"I've been thinking about her too. Want to pray for her right now?"

"Sure."

Hannah reached out and found Roxie's hand. "Heavenly Father, thank You for always taking care of us. Take care of Bev Doanne tonight wherever she is. Keep her safe. Send someone to help her. Fill her with Your peace. Let her know You love her. In Jesus' name, Amen."

"Amen," Roxie whispered. She squeezed Hannah's hand. It was good to know they could agree together in prayer and God would answer.

Hannah pulled her cover up tight under her chin and closed her eyes. Tomorrow she would tell Ezra what she'd thought she'd heard in the night. He could decide if it was anything. She turned on her side and smiled as she silently thanked God for taking care of all of them. "I love You, Heavenly Father," she said under her breath.

■

In the hidden room Bev heard Mom and Alexa sleeping with the blanket over them she'd given them earlier. Bev curled up in her blanket and closed her eyes. She slowly relaxed. A peace settled over her as if an angel were sitting beside her to keep her safe. She'd heard about angels when she'd gone to church with Mom and Alexa. Finally Dad had made them stop going. He'd said God wasn't real. In her heart Bev knew better. "You are real, God," she whispered. "I love You, no matter what Dad says."

7

Visitors

Her red hair crackling with static electricity, Chelsea flung the folded blanket down on the bed and scowled at Hannah and Roxie. "Why didn't you wake me and Kathy up last night? We wanted to go with you."

As her bright yellow hair pick moved through her blonde curls, Kathy nodded, her eyes snapping. "What if somebody had been hiding in the kitchen? Two of you might be hurt, but four of us together could've stopped anybody!"

Hannah shrugged. "I'm sorry. We thought you wouldn't want us to wake you."

"Well, you should've!" Chelsea crossed her arms and lifted her chin.

"Don't get mad at us!" Roxie stood with her fists on her hips and glared at Chelsea and Kathy. "How were we to know you'd want to go with us?"

"You should've." Chelsea flipped back her long

red hair and headed for the bedroom door. "Friends understand each other, you know."

"Then you should understand why we didn't wake you up." Roxie blocked Chelsea's way.

Hannah's stomach knotted painfully. Why were they fighting? It wasn't right for best friends to argue. Jesus wanted them to be kind to one another and to love one another. "Please don't fight any more," Hannah whispered, clasping her hands together.

Chelsea pushed Roxie aside and sailed out of the bedroom.

Kathy hesitated and followed, the yellow pick stuck in a stubborn curl. She would've liked to explore with Hannah and Roxie last night. Maybe together they could've found the secret passage.

Tears filled Hannah's black eyes. Her bottom lip quivered, and she ducked her head to keep Roxie from seeing.

Roxie flung her cover on the bed. "I can't believe those girls! You'd think we did something really terrible, but we didn't. If they want to be mad at us, I say let 'em!"

Hannah shook her head. "It's not right. Jesus says to be kind to each other. I'll be kind and love them no matter what."

"Do what you want!" Roxie strode to the door. She stopped in the doorway and faced Hannah. "If they want to be mad, then so do I!" She turned and ran downstairs.

Hannah wrapped her arms tightly across her chest as tears trickled down her cheeks. Why couldn't life be perfect? "Jesus, I need Your comfort right now," she whispered with a slight catch in her voice. "Help me know what to say so the girls won't stay mad at each other. Thank You."

A few minutes later, her heart lighter, Hannah ran downstairs and into the kitchen. The smells of coffee and toast made her hungry.

Emma looked up from where she sat at the table and smiled. She wore a green sweater that looked nice with her gray hair. "I was just ready to send Roxie after you. Have a seat and we'll have breakfast together."

Hannah smiled, hesitated a second, then sat between Chelsea and Kathy. The girls had their heads down and didn't look up until after Ezra said the blessing on the food and the day. They all ate toast and cereal in silence.

Emma frowned as she set her cup of coffee back on the saucer. "All right, girls, what's going on here? Why the long faces?"

"Whatever it is, get it settled," Ezra said gruffly.

Hannah bit her lip but didn't speak. The others didn't either.

"Roxann?" Ezra looked right at her.

She lifted her head, her cheeks bright circles of

red. "Me? Why should it be my fault? You always think if something goes wrong it's because of me!"

"Roxann!" Emma clicked her tongue. "Mind your manners!"

Roxie laced her fingers together in her lap. She couldn't look at the Best Friends. It was embarrassing to be scolded in front of them.

Hannah moved restlessly. "We had a . . . disagreement."

Ezra peered down his hook nose at her. "Over what?"

Hannah looked helplessly at the Best Friends, then blurted out, "Last night Roxie and I came downstairs to check out a noise we heard. Chelsea and Kathy thought we should've woke them up so they could be with us."

Emma's face blanched. "Ezra, could someone have come in here last night?"

Ezra shook his head. "The housekeeper has the only other key."

"Could someone pick the lock?" Hannah asked.

Roxie shivered as Chelsea and Kathy gasped.

"Tell me the whole story about last night, young lady!" Ezra dropped his napkin beside his plate and leaned toward Hannah.

She quickly told him everything. "I didn't think either of you would leave the closet door or the cupboard door open."

"We didn't," Ezra and Emma said together.

"I think someone wanted to steal the box of antiques." Hannah pushed up her sleeves and folded her hands in her lap. "Sue Monroe said a man was here, remember? And she thought his name was Galley or something like that. We found the name Marvin Deck in the Yellow Pages."

Emma's eyes widened. "I've heard of Marvin Deck! I've been told he isn't always honest in his dealings."

Ezra pushed back his chair. "I think I'll give Sue Monroe a call and ask her if the man was Marvin Deck. Then I'll check the U-Haul to make sure nobody broke into it."

"Ask Sue Monroe if she knows about the secret passage," Hannah said in a rush of words.

"Will do." Ezra leaned against the counter as he called Sue Monroe.

The Best Friends sat in silence. Maybe they'd get to walk through the secret passage even today. It would be exciting to walk the same place where runaway slaves had walked.

"No answer." Ezra hung up and rubbed his hand over his head. "I think I just might give Marvin Deck a call." Ezra grinned. "I might be able to outfox the fox—if he's the one who stopped by to talk to Sue Monroe. We really don't know if he was."

Before Ezra could use the phone, the front doorbell rang. Everyone jumped even though the sound was melodious and not at all frightening. Then the girls giggled, and Emma patted her cheeks as if to settle her nerves.

Ezra started across the kitchen. "I'll get it."

The Best Friends looked at each other, then jumped up and hurried after Ezra.

Emma followed. "I don't want to be left out of anything either."

Her hair combed neatly and her makeup done nicely, Sue Monroe stood at the door, her large purse over her arm. "I was driving past, and I suddenly remembered that antique dealer's name."

"Marvin Deck?" Emma asked.

Sue's eyes widened and she nodded as she stepped inside. "How did you know? Did he come here again?"

Ezra explained how the girls had guessed the man's name. "Emma says he's not always honest."

Sue nodded. "I know I didn't trust him at all."

Hannah took a half a step forward. "We know there's a secret passage in the house. Do you know where it is?"

"We thought Lenny might've told you," Ezra said.

Sue flushed and tried desperately to think of what to say without lying. "He did talk about it, but he said he liked keeping it a secret."

Ezra loomed over Sue. "So, he didn't tell you?"

She thought quickly. "Didn't he tell you? You're family."

"He didn't. The girls want to try to find the secret passage. I looked for years, but I didn't find it."

"Maybe the girls will," Sue said with a nervous laugh. "I must be going. I did want to borrow a rake from the shed. I'll bring it back later today."

"Sure. Go right ahead." Ezra opened the door, letting in crisp fresh air.

Sue hurried toward the shed, her heart lodged in her mouth. She'd seen Jim Doanne watching her house this morning and had had a hard time losing him. She'd driven into an open garage two blocks from her house, watched him zoom past, then backed out before the people in the house could question her. Then she drove out of town as quickly as she could.

Now, inside the shed Sue pressed the appropriate post, walked through the secret door, closed it, and clicked on her flashlight. She hurried through the tunnel, shored up with wooden beams. Sand sprinkled down from the top. The floor was hard-packed dirt. She ran up the wooden steps to the door that led to the secret room behind the closet, opened it cautiously, and whispered, "It's me. Don't be scared."

"Oh, Mom!" Mallary's eyes looked wide in her ashen face as she jumped up from the folding chair.

A lantern burned in a corner, shedding a soft glow of light in the tiny room. Alexa and Bev sat on the wooden floor with their backs against three blankets piled in a corner. The room smelled closed in.

"We must be very quiet." Sue set her huge purse on the floor. "The others are probably in the kitchen again, but they might still be in the living room."

"Why can't we go with you today?" Bev asked.

"You know why!" Sue pulled three bananas, three pints of milk, and three sweet rolls from her purse, as well as a box of crackers and a large can of tomato soup. "The others will be going back to their own homes today, so tonight you can fix your own supper and sleep in beds again."

Bev wanted to refuse the food, but she was too hungry. She stuck a straw in the small carton of milk and sipped it. It was warm, but it had to do. If she were home, she'd be eating pancakes swimming in maple syrup, bacon, eggs, and a tall glass of icy cold milk.

Sue sat on the folding chair and looked up at Mallary as she ate. "Jim was watching my house this morning."

Mallary almost choked on the bite of roll. "Oh, Mom! Did he follow you?"

"Yes, but I lost him."

As Sue talked, Bev forced down her food. It was her fault Dad was watching Grandma's house. Bev chewed the last of her sweet roll. It suddenly tasted like a cardboard cutout of a roll. She shouldn't have phoned Dad last night. Maybe he had followed Grandma—and maybe he would find them! Bev shivered. Had Dad believed her last night when she said she'd become the perfect daughter? If not, he'd go on being mean to them. Bev forced back a sob.

Several minutes later Sue hurried through the passage to the shed and back out into the morning sunshine. She started outdoors, then remembered to lift the rake off the wall to carry to her car. She couldn't forget why she was supposedly here, in case someone was watching.

Inside the house Hannah watched Sue drive away. She frowned thoughtfully. Why had it taken Sue so long just to get a rake?

Roxie stepped to the window beside Hannah. "What are you looking at?"

"Sue Monroe just left."

"So?"

"She took a long time getting that rake."

"Hannah, you're suspicious of everything!"

"I know. It's my nature as a mystery lover." Hannah chuckled.

"Ezra finally got ahold of Marvin Deck."

The laugh died in Hannah's throat. "And?"

"Ezra and Grandma are going to town to see him and see if he happens to have something of Lenny's on display in his shop."

"While they're gone, we'll keep looking for the secret passage."

"Good idea." Roxie sighed heavily. "I wish Chelsea and Kathy would get over being mad at us."

"They will." Hannah pushed her hands deep into the pockets of her jeans. "Let's go talk to them and see that they do."

Chelsea and Kathy were upstairs in the bedroom no one had slept in. They looked at the bed, then at each other. Something was very wrong. Chelsea turned as the door opened.

"Look at this." Chelsea pointed to the bed. The spread was pulled to one side, and the pillows weren't in their usual place.

Roxie blew out her breath.

Hannah touched the bed. "Someone pulled the blankets off. It wasn't me."

"Not me," the others said together.

"It's another mystery." Hannah fingered the end of her ponytail. "Before we try to solve it, can we please . . . make up?" She looked pleadingly at Chelsea and Kathy. "We don't want you mad at us."

"I'm not mad any longer." Chelsea turned to Kathy. "Are you?"

Kathy shook her head. "But next time, wake us up!"

"We will!" Hannah and Roxie promised.

The Best Friends laughed together because that's what Best Friends did.

Several minutes later Ezra and Emma drove away, and the Best Friends stood in the yard beside the U-Haul trailer. Quacking ducks flew overhead in a big V.

"Where should we look first?" Kathy asked, her eyes sparkling with excitement.

"The shed." Hannah studied the shed thoughtfully. "Maybe the corner is free of cobwebs because that's the exit of the secret passage."

Roxie trembled. Was she ready to find the secret passage? It suddenly seemed too terrifying.

Just then two girls and a boy rode up on bikes. The Best Friends watched them and were surprised that they knew them—brother and sister Austin and Kris Coltrain and their cousin Heather Axelrod.

Roxie flushed to the roots of her short dark hair. For a whole week now she'd loved eighth grader Austin Coltrain—the best week of Roxie's life. He wasn't the best looking boy Roxie knew, but there was just something about him that made her heart do flipflops. Last week when she'd put the carving of her baby skunk in her special art display at school, Austin had stopped beside her and watched.

"You do excellent work, Roxie."

"Thank you." He knew her name! And he'd talked to her even though she was only a sixth grader!

"I wish I could carve."

"You should try it. You might be able to do it."
His blue eyes had melted her on the spot. Now, she
found it hard to breathe with him right there in the
same yard.

His sister Kris was in sixth grade with Roxie,
and they'd become friends, mainly because Roxie
loved Austin. Heather was in sixth grade too. She
had to take special reading, and many of the kids
made fun of her. But Roxie hadn't, not even before
she knew Heather was Austin's cousin.

Chelsea smiled. "Hi."

Austin dropped his bike in the grass. He had
short brown hair and wore jeans and a blue sweatshirt. "You're trespassing! We know you girls don't
live here."

"We're helping Ezra Menski take out his
uncle's things," Hannah said.

"Lenny Menski went to Arizona." Heather laid
her bike near Austin's. She and Kris looked more
like sisters than cousins.

"We know he did," Roxie said. "He sold his
place and decided to stay with his daughter."

"He did?" Kris asked in surprise. "That's too
bad."

"We'll miss him." Austin glanced around the
place. "He told great stories about helping slaves get
to freedom before and during the Civil War. He said
he found a diary from the man who built the
house."

The Best Friends almost shouted with excitement. "Did he tell you where the secret passage is?" they asked all together.

Kris and Heather giggled.

Austin grinned. "Did you practice that?" He hunched his shoulders. "He didn't tell us, but he gave us a lot of hints."

"Tell us!"

Austin shook his head. "No way! We want to find it on our own, and if we tell you girls, you might find it first."

"We know you've been looking," Kris said. "We saw lights on in the house the past five nights."

Hannah's eyes widened. Last night had been their only night! Who had been in the house the other nights?

"We decided to come today to check out who was here," Heather said. "We even thought about calling the police because we knew Mr. Menski was in Arizona."

The Best Friends looked at each other excitedly. There really was a mystery to solve! Somehow they'd solve it before they went home tonight—danger or not!

8

Another Search

Hannah ran to the back of the U-Haul. "It's locked, and the diary's in there!" She thumped her hand on the padlocked door. "I helped Ezra carry all of Lenny's important documents out here yesterday. If only we'd known about the diary!"

Kris rattled the padlock. "When will Ezra Menski be back?"

"Before noon." Roxie smiled a tiny smile at Austin. Inside she was smiling from ear to ear. Nothing seemed important to her but Austin.

He smiled at her, then looked quickly away.

"We were planning to check in the shed for a hidden door or something," Kathy said. "Want to go with us?"

Roxie decided then and there she'd never get mad at Kathy again. As unobtrusively as she could, Roxie fell into step beside Austin. She wasn't brave enough to be obvious about liking Austin, just in case he rejected her. She listened as the others gave their ideas on the secret passage—what it would look like and where it would be.

Heather chuckled softly. "I even thought it might be in an old tree stump at the edge of the woods. But it wasn't."

"I looked in the barn lots of times," Austin said. "I couldn't find anything. Lenny sure laughed. He said to keep trying."

Just as they reached the shed a red car stopped near the U-Haul. It was Jim Doanne.

"He's looking for Bev," Hannah said in a low voice as they all turned to head back to the driveway.

"He stopped at our house too." Kris sounded angry. "I told him I wouldn't tell him where she was even if I knew!"

"I did too!" Heather knotted her fists at her sides. She lived down the road from her cousins.

The Best Friends stopped and looked in surprise at Kris and Heather. "Why are you mad at Jim Doanne?"

Heather glanced over at the driveway, where Jim Doanne was getting out of his car. "I think he beats Bev. I asked her and she said he didn't, but she came to school lots of times with bruises. She couldn't even wear her swimsuit because of bruises!"

"That's terrible!" Chelsea wanted to run to Jim Doanne and demand that he leave.

"We don't know for sure he beats her," Austin said in a low voice. "Dad checked into it and couldn't learn anything." Austin turned to Roxie. "Dad works for Children's Services."

Roxie wanted to hear everything about Austin, but she forced her attention back to the dreaded visitor.

"I'm back again," Jim Doanne called as he hurried toward them. He wore a green and black sweater, tan pants, and brown leather slip-on shoes. He looked tired and unhappy.

The kids didn't say anything until he reached them, and then Hannah said, "We still haven't seen Bev."

"I know her grandma was here this morning." Jim Doanne's jaw tightened, and fire flashed from his eyes. "And don't tell me differently! Did she come to see Bev?"

Kathy knotted her fists at her sides. "Nobody was here this morning but Sue Monroe, Lenny Menski's housekeeper."

"She's my wife's mother—my daughters' grandmother."

The Best Friends gasped in surprise. Maybe Bev Doanne was hiding in the hidden room!

"What did Sue do while she was here?" Jim Doanne asked, his gaze piercing each one, one at a time, like they were germs on a glass slide under a microscope.

Hannah opened her mouth to say something, but Kris nudged her.

Austin stepped forward. "They don't have to tell you anything, Mr. Doanne. And you don't have any right to ask them!"

The Best Friends looked at Austin in disbelief. How did he dare to speak that way to an attorney even if he did beat his daughter?

Jim Doanne shook his finger at Austin. "You're treading on dangerous territory, boy."

"And you're trespassing!"

"I'll find Bev, and nothing you can do will stop me!" Jim Doanne turned on his heels and rushed angrily to his car. Gravel spewed out behind his tires as he sped away.

Roxie trembled. "He does have a temper, doesn't he?"

Kris shivered. "I know he beats Bev. I hope he never finds her!"

Her eyes wide, Chelsea pressed her hand to her throat. "But she's his daughter. What if she's all alone and scared?"

"Maybe her grandma does know where she is." Heather looked thoughtfully toward the house. "Somebody's been in Lenny's house the past five days. Maybe it was Bev."

"All alone?" Roxie shivered. "That's too scary!"

"We found a work sheet for that awful book, *The Truth About Helen*, in one of the bedrooms." Hannah hated to even say the title of the book. "It could've been Bev's."

Kathy nodded. "We even said that, then laughed at the ridiculous idea. It's sure not ridiculous now, is it?"

"But we still don't know for sure." Hannah knew they'd jumped to a conclusion without proof. "We can't assume Bev is here."

"She could be though." Austin headed for the shed. "Let's see what we can find in there."

Roxie ran after him. Her heart was leaping with happiness when she should've been concerned about the missing Bev Doanne. She smiled. She couldn't help feeling happy, could she? Austin was here. If she had her way, she'd invite him and the girls to stay for the picnic they'd planned for lunch.

In the shed Hannah pointed out the spot that was free of cobwebs. "Let's concentrate on that area. Maybe we'll find a hidden door."

"I know from Lenny's stories that the secret passage was well concealed." Austin ran a hand lightly over the wall. "If anyone was caught helping runaway slaves, they were put to death by hanging or flogging."

"How awful!" Bitter bile filled Roxie's mouth,

and she stepped away from the wall as she pictured a man being hung or whipped to death for helping another man escape to freedom.

Austin squared his shoulders and stood tall. "If I lived back then, I'd hide a runaway even if it was dangerous to me. And I'll help Bev Doanne any way I can!"

Suddenly Roxie felt the same way. She wanted to stand at Austin's side and declare her feelings, but she stayed near the lawn mower, agreeing with him secretly.

Hannah peered closer at the wall as she carefully ran her hand over every square inch of the clean area. She couldn't reach the ceiling, but she didn't think a hidden catch would be that high.

Several minutes later they gave up their search and walked slowly back outdoors. The sun seemed extra-bright after being in the shed. Just then the sound of a bell drifted across the field.

"We have to get home," Kris said. "That's our mom ringing for us. We'll try to come back later."

"Please do!" Roxie looked right at Austin.

He smiled at her. "We will."

The Best Friends said good-bye and stood in the yard until Austin and the girls reached the end of the driveway on their bikes. Roxie sighed heavily.

"He's sooo nice!"

"He sure is." Hannah grinned at Roxie. "I think you think he's nicer than the rest of us do."

"Why didn't you tell us you like him?" Chelsea asked.

"I thought we didn't keep secrets from each other." Hannah stopped short. She hadn't told them about the pickle dish. *She'd* kept a secret from the Best Friends!

"What's wrong?" Chelsea looked closely at Hannah. "You look like you're going to cry."

Hannah bit her lip, then burst out with the story about the pickle dish. "I didn't want to keep the secret from you, but I was too ashamed to tell you. How can I tell Mom the truth after letting her blame the twins?"

Roxie frowned. "Why even tell? Your mom thinks it's settled."

Kathy jabbed Roxie's arm. "She can't keep quiet! It's like telling a lie."

Roxie flushed. She sometimes forgot how important it was to be like Jesus. "So, how can she tell?"

"With God's help," Chelsea said softly. "You know that, Hannah."

"I know, but I guess I forgot. Some things seem harder to do than others."

"Think of Bev Doanne." Kathy shook her head. "She has a lot more to think about than telling the truth about a pickle dish."

Hannah nodded. "I know. It always seems like

your own troubles are a lot worse than other people's."

Chelsea bit her bottom lip. "That's true. I have to find a way to tell Mr. Borgman I won't read *The Truth About Helen*. He'll be sooo mad! And I know he'll give me a failing mark for the day. It's just not fair!"

Hannah glanced off across the yard, then back at Chelsea. "Getting a failing grade with Mr. Borgman isn't as bad as reading a book that's too dirty to read."

"I know." Chelsea moved restlessly. "But I hate getting a failing mark! It'll pull my grade for the marking period down to a B!"

"I think we should talk to the principal and teachers in a special meeting the way you and Kesha did, Chel." Kathy looked very determined. "It might make a difference."

Chelsea's heart leaped. Why hadn't she thought of that? "I think you're right, Kathy! We could all call a meeting with Mr. Borgman and Mrs. Evans and tell them how we feel about the book!"

Roxie jumped right in with her idea. "We'll talk to other kids who refuse to read it because it's bad and see if they'll go with us. We'll ask kids who go to our church tomorrow, then others at school Monday morning. We'll have a meeting Monday and take care of it."

"Yes!" Chelsea twirled around the yard,

silently thanking God for the answer to her problem.

They talked a while longer, then ran inside to look for the secret passage.

"Let's have a soda first," Kathy said as she headed for the kitchen. She opened the refrigerator. "Hey! Who drank all the pop?"

"Not me for sure," Chelsea said. She didn't drink pop and usually chose apple juice instead.

Hannah looked in the refrigerator. "Another mystery!" She laughed right out loud. "I wonder what else is gone." She looked for the bag of oranges and found them in the bottom drawer of the refrigerator.

Shivering, Roxie turned from the cupboard. "The cookies are gone."

"I wonder if Bev does know where the secret passage is," Chelsea whispered as she darted a look around. "Could she really be hiding right here in this house?"

"It's sure possible," Kathy said.

Hannah flung her arms wide. "I have a fantastic idea!"

"What?"

"Let's go in every room in the house and shout to Bev."

Kathy patted her racing heart. "What'll we say?"

"We'll say, 'Bev, we want to help you. Come out so we can talk!' Maybe she'll come out."

"Let's go!" Chelsea headed for the utility room. She cupped her hands around her mouth and shouted, "Bev, we want to help you! Come out so we can talk!" Chelsea waited with the Best Friends pressed tightly against her. Nothing happened, so they walked back to the kitchen.

"Let me do it." Roxie shouted the same words. She giggled. "I feel stupid."

"If we help Bev, it doesn't matter how stupid we feel." Hannah hurried to the living room. Before she could shout, Kathy did.

They stepped into the walk-in closet, and Hannah took her turn to shout to Bev. To make double-sure Bev heard if she were hiding nearby, Hannah shouted again.

■

Behind the wall Bev jumped and bit back a scream. How did the girls even know she was there? Mom and Alexa would be in hysterics if they'd heard. They'd gone down the passage to get fresh air outside the shed. Bev locked her icy hands together. How she longed to open the secret door. Her heart pounded so loudly, she was sure the girls could hear it. Dare she talk to them? They said they wanted to help. They knew how to pray, and they believed God answered prayer.

Bev frowned. How did they know she needed

help? How had they learned she was hiding there? She shivered and reached to open the secret door.

Just then Mallary and Alexa stepped into the hidden room, saw Bev reach for the secret door, and heard someone calling to her.

Mallary caught Bev and jerked her back. "Don't!" she hissed in Bev's ear. "Please don't!"

"Bev, we can't let Dad find us," Alexa whispered tearfully.

Bev strained against her mom. "But they want to help us."

"We can't trust them." Mallary pulled Bev tight against her. "We just can't! We don't dare trust anyone. You have to understand."

Bev slowly relaxed and leaned against her mom. "I'm sorry . . . I'm sorry . . . I just want to go home."

"I know . . . I know."

Bev buried her face in her mom's neck and sobbed.

The Picnic

Upstairs in the last room the Best Friends sank to the floor in a circle and looked at each other.

"Maybe Bev's not here." Chelsea wrapped her arms around her knees. She smelled the faint aroma of lemon furniture polish. "She could be miles away . . . Or even hiding at her grandma's."

Roxie leaned forward, a worried look on her face. "What if she *is* in the hidden passage, and what if she's hurt and can't answer?"

"That would be too terrible!" Kathy shook her head hard. "I don't want to even think about that!"

"Not thinking about it or thinking about it doesn't change the facts," Hannah said briskly. "You can't expect something to stop being what it is just because you put it out of your mind. Like the starving people in the world—whether we think about them or not, they are still starving." Hannah took a deep breath. "So, instead of pushing thoughts of things like that away, we can pray for the starving people, pray for sick people, pray for kids who get beat or molested by their parents. That's what we can do to make a difference in all those terrible things."

"You're right." Chelsea nodded solemnly. "We prayed for Bev before, and we can keep on praying for her."

"Right!" they said together.

Once again they prayed for Bev and her family, then slowly walked downstairs to the kitchen.

Hannah leaned against the counter and looked at the phone. "I wonder if Bev's mom knows where she is. Maybe we should call her."

"I put Jim Doanne's card in the drawer with the phone book." Chelsea pointed to the drawer directly in front of Hannah. "The card has his home number on it."

Hannah pulled out the card and punched the numbers. "It's ringing." She rolled her eyes. "Answering machine." She listened to the message, then hung up before the beep.

"Try Sue Monroe," Kathy suggested from where she sat at the table drinking a glass of water. Roxie sat beside her with her hands locked together on the table.

Hannah found the number written in the back of the phone book and called Sue Monroe. She answered immediately.

"Mrs. Monroe, this is Hannah Shigwam. I'm helping at Lenny Menski's."

"What's wrong? Did something happen?"

Hannah heard the panic in Sue's voice and wondered about it. "Do you know where your daughter, Mrs. Doanne, is?"

Sue gasped, then cautiously asked, "Why do you want to know?"

Hannah frowned thoughtfully. "Jim Doanne was here again asking about Bev. We're wondering if she could be hidden in the secret passage. We want to help her."

"That's very nice of you." Sue's brain whirled with what to say to put the girls off Bev's track. Suddenly she knew the right words. "Please don't worry about Bev. Her mother and sister will take care of her."

Hannah leaned heavily on the counter. "Is she with them?"

"Of course!"

"Does her dad know?"

Sue hesitated. "I don't want to talk about him." She cleared her throat. "I've got to go. Thanks for calling. Bev will be glad to know someone her own age cares."

Slowly Hannah hung up the receiver. "I could be wrong, but if Bev really is here, then so are her mother and sister."

With loud exclamations of surprise, the Best

Friends clustered around Hannah. She told them what Sue Monroe had said.

"It would really be terrible if they all were here hiding in a tiny dark room. With the mice!" Roxie shuddered. "I'd hate to hide away like that!"

Kathy brushed tears from her eyes. "I want to help them. The minute Ezra gets back, we'll look in the diary and see where the secret passage is."

"You know we might be wrong about them being here," Chelsea said softly.

Hannah nodded. "Chel's right. But just in case, we'll keep looking for them. And we'll keep praying for them!"

Several minutes later they heard Ezra drive up. They rushed out to meet him, all talking at once.

Laughing, Emma held up her hand. "Girls, one at a time. What in the world has got you so excited?"

They took turns talking and soon had the story told about their suspicions and what the neighbor kids who'd come over had said.

Roxie forced back a flush at just hearing Austin mentioned.

"What a miserable turn of events!" Emma cried.

With a long, troubled sigh Ezra shook his head. "And there's no way we can help, none that I know about. Lenny took the diary with him," he said.

Ezra spread his hands wide. "We don't have a map to lead us to the secret passage."

The girls groaned, and Emma clicked her tongue.

Emma slipped her hand through Ezra's arm. "What about the new owners? Did Lenny tell them about the secret passage?"

"He might have, but I don't know who the people are."

"We keep hitting dead ends, don't we?" Emma tugged on Ezra's arm and smiled at the girls. "Right now we're going to the woods for a picnic. We'll put aside all our concerns and have fun. I brought a bucket of chicken and other good things to eat. They're in the back of the station wagon, so each of you carry something and let's go."

Several minutes later they sat deep in the woods on a blanket with the food in the center. A stream rushed over the rocks beside them. Birds sang, and a squirrel chattered noisily. The air smelled of fried chicken, pine trees, and the water in the stream. The Best Friends laughed and talked and listened to Emma's jokes and Ezra's stories about when he was a boy.

Roxie savored her last bite of chicken. The crispy outside was her favorite part. She wiped her mouth and fingers with a white paper napkin, thankful Austin wasn't there to see how messy she got from eating chicken. She glanced over her shoulder, then froze. Jim Doanne was watching them! He ducked quickly out of sight behind a huge oak. She tried to speak but couldn't. She jabbed Chelsea's arm and pointed to the oak.

"What? What did you see?" Chelsea saw the terror on Roxie's face, and her skin pricked with fear.

"What's wrong?" Her eyes wide, Kathy looked all around. She didn't see anything frightening.

Hannah jumped up, ready for whatever came.

"Roxann, what's wrong?" Emma said sharply.

"Jim Doanne," Roxie managed to whisper. "Behind that tree."

"I'll handle this!" Ezra pushed himself up and strode toward the tree. "Jim Doanne, you might as well show yourself! Roxann spotted you there. Come out right now!"

The Best Friends stood with Emma and watched and waited. Would Jim Doanne run away or would he face Ezra? A blue jay screeched, and another answered. Finally Jim Doanne stepped into sight. His face was ashen, and a twig clung to his brown hair.

"I thought Bev was with you," Jim said lamely.

"She's not." Ezra crossed his arms and peered down his nose at Jim. "Anything else?"

Jim hung his head.

Emma stepped forward. "Ezra, honey, please don't be gruff. The man is very upset." She walked to Jim and touched his hand. "Walk back to the house with us. We'll help if we can."

The Best Friends flashed looks of astonishment at each other, then scowled at Emma. Why would she want to help such a terrible man? She'd heard what they'd said about him.

Jim Doanne brushed tears from his eyes. "I don't know if I can live another day like this."

"God loves you, Mr. Doanne," Emma said gently. "He wants to help you."

Jim jerked away from Emma, and his face darkened with anger. "Don't talk to me about God! My father used to do that as he beat me with his belt. I don't want anything to do with God!"

"He loves you anyway." Emma smiled. "He wants you to be happy and productive and at peace. He wants to forgive you and make you into a new person."

Jim swore and stormed away along the path that led back to the house.

"He's a real jerk!" Roxie snapped.

Emma turned on her. "No, he is not! He has problems, and he does things he shouldn't do, but God says to love Jim Doanne."

The Best Friends knew that was true, but it was hard to do it when they thought about Bev. Slowly they cleaned up the picnic stuff, rolled up the blanket, and followed Emma and Ezra back to the house. Jim Doanne's car still stood in the yard, but he wasn't in sight. Emma and Ezra stopped beside it.

Hannah turned to the Best Friends and whispered in alarm, "What if he's inside? What if he found the secret passage?"

Chelsea's face turned as white as the clouds in the sky, making her freckles stand out boldly. "Maybe he'll beat Bev right in the hidden room where no one can stop him."

Kathy and Roxie gasped and ran toward the house. It would be terrible if Jim Doanne found Bev and beat her!

Hannah burst through the door with Chelsea, Roxie, and Kathy right behind her. "Bev!" they shouted together.

They stopped and stared at each other. Kathy whispered, "She might not even be here. Then what? We'd be shouting for no reason!"

Slowly they carried the picnic things to the kitchen and set them on the table. The aroma of fried chicken drifted up from the container.

Just then Kathy saw that the light on the phone was blinking. Someone was using another phone in the house. Her heart hammering, she slapped Hannah's back and speechlessly pointed at the light.

"Someone else is in the house," Hannah whispered. They knew there was a phone in Lenny's study and another in the master bedroom. "Two of us can go upstairs and two to the study to look."

Hannah turned to Chelsea. "We'll go upstairs. Roxie and Kathy, check the study. Be very careful in case it's not Bev."

"It could be Marvin Deck." Kathy's voice broke.

"Even if it is, he's probably not dangerous." Hannah sounded very businesslike, but inside she was shaking worse than a dish of warm jello.

Hannah and Chelsea crept silently upstairs to the master bedroom. The door stood open halfway. They looked at each other, then together pushed against it, swinging it almost back against the wall. The bed was made neatly. Emma's overnight bag sat on a bench at the foot of the bed. The full-length mirror flashed back a reflection of the girls. No one was in the room. The phone sat on a nightstand beside the king-sized bed. Nobody was using it.

"Downstairs . . . quick!" Hannah gripped Chelsea's hand and tugged her toward the stairs. They were just starting down when Roxie and Kathy started up.

"No one was in the room," all four said together.

Hannah stopped short. "Quick! Search the rooms!" She pulled Chelsea around, and they raced to the bedroom.

Roxie and Kathy turned just in time to see a flash of color as someone ran into the walk-in closet. The door closed with a snap. Someone had probably been using the phone in the study, had hidden from them, then ran to the closet when he or she felt safe. But now whoever was hiding in the closet couldn't get out without them catching him or her.

"Hannah!" Kathy shouted, her feet rooted to the spot.

"Chelsea!" Roxie screamed, unable to move even a step.

Hannah and Chelsea shot down the stairs. "What's wrong?"

Roxie and Kathy pointed toward the closet. "Someone went in it," Kathy whispered.

Hannah ran across the living room and reached for the doorknob. Her hand trembled. Silently she prayed for the courage to face whoever was in the closet. She jerked the closet door open and clicked on the light, expecting to see someone. Instead she saw empty shelves and empty space. "It's empty! Nobody's in here."

"But someone went in there!" Kathy looked around Hannah, sure she'd see someone. "It *is* empty!"

"There must be a secret door in here some-where." Chelsea wanted to rush into the closet and start looking, but she couldn't summon up enough courage.

"I'll get Grandma and Ezra." Roxie's mouth felt almost too dry for the words she spoke. She stumbled to the front door and opened it.

"Grandma! Ezra! Come here!" Roxie's heart sank. They weren't standing in the yard. The station wagon and Jim Doanne's car were both there. Roxie spun around to face the Best Friends. "Grandma's gone! And Ezra!"

"Maybe they went to the barn."

"Or the shed."

"They wouldn't leave without telling us."

Roxie bit her lip. "Unless somebody made them. Jim Doanne was really really mad."

Hannah looked in the closet again, then toward the front door. She'd wanted to search until she found the secret door, but she knew they had to find Ezra and Emma. "We'd better go look for them."

The Best Friends agreed and hurried outdoors. Warm wind blew dust across a bare field. Austin, Kris, and Heather were riding their bikes up the driveway. Happy for help, the Best Friends ran to meet them.

Austin dropped his bike at the side of the driveway. "What's wrong? I see Jim Doanne is here again."

Roxie quickly told Austin and the girls what had happened since they'd left. "We're out here to look for my grandma and Ezra. I just hope Jim Doanne didn't hurt them."

Chelsea ran toward the barn. "Let's check the barn first, then the shed."

Roxie ran beside Austin, while Kris and

Heather ran next to Hannah and Kathy. They all reached the barn at the same time.

"Grandma?" Roxie looked around the dim interior of the barn. She smelled musty hay. Dust particles danced in the sunlight that came streaming in through cracks in the walls and roof. A cat meowed and ran behind an old bale of hay.

Hannah glanced up the ladder that led to the haymow. "Ezra? Emma?" No answer. "I don't think they'd go up there, but we have to check everywhere."

Austin quickly climbed the ladder and looked across the dusty haymow. "They aren't up here."

Roxie watched Austin climb down. Just seeing him made her tingle all over even though she was worried about her grandma.

Chelsea led the way outdoors and across the grass to the shed. Sweat popped out on her forehead. She waited until everyone reached the shed, then slid the door open on its tracks with a loud rumble. No one was inside.

Roxie groaned. "Do you think they went back to the woods?"

"Maybe they found the secret passage and are in it . . . with Jim Doanne," Austin said in a low, tight voice.

"I'm going to check the woods." Hannah ran to the path they'd taken into the forest. She heard the others following her, but she didn't look back.

Silently she prayed for Emma and Ezra. She ran into the shade of the trees and looked deep into the woods. She didn't see anyone. She thought of what Emma had told Jim Doanne. Finally Hannah prayed for him. It made her feel better.

"Where could they be?" Kris asked in a worried voice.

Roxie turned to Austin. "You know the area. Where could they be that we couldn't see them and they couldn't hear us?"

Austin shrugged. "Nowhere . . . Unless they walked across the road to the Wilson place. You can see a part of the house through the trees."

Relief made Roxie's legs tremble. It sounded very logical. "Maybe they *are* there. Let's go look."

"Why not phone the Wilsons instead?" Kris asked.

"Good idea!" Hannah smiled at Kris, then ran to the house with the others. Kris told her the number, and Hannah called.

Chelsea filled a glass with water and sipped it to relieve the dryness of her mouth and throat as she listened to Hannah ask about Ezra and Emma.

"They are there." Hannah replaced the receiver and smiled in relief. "Jim Doanne is too. The Wilsons think they saw Bev."

Austin knotted his fists. "I hope Jim Doanne doesn't find her!"

Roxie wanted to say something to comfort Austin, but she didn't know what to say.

Just then a door slammed somewhere in the house.

Roxie jumped closer to Austin as the others stared at the kitchen door.

Who had slammed the door? Was a dangerous person lurking in the house? Or was it Bev waiting to ask for their help?

10

Marvin Deck

Austin led the way out of the kitchen, and the others cautiously followed. Roxie stayed as close to Austin as she could.

In the living room Hannah whispered, "We'd better split up to look or whoever it is might get away."

Roxie flushed as she stepped closer to Austin. Why hadn't she noticed how black and long his lashes were? Or how cute he looked when he was being so intense. "I'll go with you, Austin."

He smiled. "Good." He turned to the others. "Kris and Kathy, go together. Heather, you go with Chelsea and Hannah. Is that okay with everyone?"

They all nodded as they teamed up the way Austin had said.

Roxie tried not to look too happy. This was serious business, and she needed to remember that—somehow. She tugged her sweatshirt over her jeans, then pushed the long sleeves up to her elbows. She was ready for anything!

Hannah started for the stairs. "We'll check upstairs. Shout if you find someone. We'll do the same."

"*Scream* is more like it," Chelsea muttered as she hurried after Hannah.

"I'm coming too!" Heather ran after Hannah and Chelsea.

"We'll take the front part of the house," Austin said. "You girls take the back."

Kathy smiled shakily at Kris as they hurried off to check the bathroom, family room, and den. The dining room was also in their part of the house, but with one quick glance they could see no one was hiding in there.

In the bathroom Kris pulled aside the flowered shower curtain, then giggled. "I was afraid somebody was hiding in the tub. It's a good thing nobody was or I'd have fainted right on the spot."

"I know what you mean." Kathy opened the linen closet. The shelves were empty, and there wasn't room even for a little kid to hide. "I'd be really scared if we did find someone."

Kris nodded. "But it would be so exciting too!" She wrinkled her nose. "It seems like Austin always has all the fun. Do you have brothers?"

"Yes. Duke . . . And a foster brother, Brody.

They stay busy practicing their guitars most of the time when they're home."

"I know them! I didn't realize they were your brothers. Brody's sooo cute!"

Kathy giggled. "I guess he is. I never really noticed."

"I know what you mean. Girls say Austin is cute, but he's not to me. Bev Doanne really thinks so."

Kathy stiffened. "Bev likes Austin?"

Kris nodded. "They go together."

Kathy's stomach knotted. What would Roxie do when she found out? "We'd better keep looking."

Kris led the way to the den. They looked behind the leather sofa and even in a built-in unit of shelves. They hurried to the family room and peeked inside the closet. There wasn't anyplace to hide in there.

"I wonder if the secret passage is behind this wall." Kathy ran a hand over the wall but didn't find a secret release or anything like that.

Upstairs Hannah, Chelsea, and Heather looked under the bed in each room, in closets, and in bathrooms. They listened intently in case someone shouted. Hannah wanted to be the one to find the intruder.

"I hope it's Bev," Heather whispered. "If she knew Austin was looking for her, she'd let him find her."

Chelsea turned to Heather in surprise, afraid to learn what she really meant. "How come?"

Heather looked from Chelsea to Hannah. "Didn't you know? They go together. Bev and Austin."

Hannah's heart dropped to her feet. Roxie would be crushed when she learned the truth.

Chelsea wanted to ask all the details about Austin and Bev, but she didn't. Somehow they'd have to tell Roxie the truth. But they'd have to do it when Austin wasn't around to see her despair. Chelsea and Hannah exchanged looks, knowing they were both thinking the same thing. They had to protect Roxie. That's what best friends did.

In the front part of the house Austin stopped Roxie just inside the guest bedroom. He put his finger to his lips for silence, then motioned for her to look under the bed while he checked the closet and the adjoining bathroom.

Roxie walked softly across the rose-colored carpet, then knelt down and lifted up the flowered dust ruffle. If someone had been hiding under the bed, she'd have screamed her head off. But no one was there, and she breathed a big sigh of relief. She'd feel a whole lot better if she were within touching distance of Austin.

Across the room Austin stepped out of the closet. "It's empty." He sounded disappointed. "Let's check the study next."

Roxie walked close beside Austin to Lenny Menski's study. She peeked at Austin and smiled. Probably the wind had blown a door shut. Probably nobody was lurking inside. But she really didn't care if someone was there or not. The search had given her time alone with Austin. She wished she could've talked to him, but being with him even though they had to keep quiet was better than nothing. One of these days they'd have a chance to talk and she could say all the things she wanted to say to him, then listen to all the things he wanted to say to her. Maybe he'd visit her, and they could walk to the park together or something. Mom and Dad wouldn't let her go out with boys yet, but they allowed boys to come over. They'd like Austin. He was the kind of boy they'd let her go with when she was old enough.

Austin opened the study door. He wanted Bev to be there, but she wasn't. Lenny's big desk stood in front of a wall lined with windows. A red leather couch sat across the room from the desk. The closet door stood open.

Roxie shivered and suddenly didn't want to follow Austin into the room, but of course she did. It would be terrible if he knew what a coward she was. She stayed at his side as he looked behind the desk, then in the closet. The room was empty.

Just then she caught movement from the corner of her eye. She clutched Austin's arm.

He looked at her questioningly, then followed her gaze. He didn't see anything. "What?" he whispered.

She swallowed hard and tried to calm her racing heart. She'd probably imagined the movement. Slowly she walked so she could see behind the open door. She'd been right! A man dressed in a gray suit stood there. He was about forty years old with graying brown hair and hazel eyes. Roxie screamed at the top of her lungs. She hadn't meant to scream—it just happened. She wondered what Austin would think of her, but she kept screaming anyway.

The man stepped from behind the door and shook his finger at Roxie. "Stop it! Right now!"

Roxie gulped and stopped screaming, but she gripped Austin's hand so tightly her own hand hurt.

"What are you doing here? Who are you?" Austin demanded.

"I might ask you the same." The man scowled at Austin and Roxie. "You neither one live here, so why are you here?"

"We don't have to answer to you." Austin didn't look or sound a bit frightened. Roxie was very proud of him. She was so scared, she didn't know if she could stand up a minute longer.

"I'll be on my way and let the police deal with you." The man started out just as Hannah blocked the doorway, the others crowding behind her.

"Are you Marvin Deck?" Hannah asked accusingly.

The man nodded with a surprised look. "Now, let me pass! I'm in a hurry."

"You're going to wait right here in this house until Ezra Menski talks to you." Chelsea sounded firm even though she was shivery inside.

"There's no need for that," Deck snapped.

"Oh, yes there is! We'll wait in the living room." Hannah led the way with her back stiff and her head high.

Roxie stayed close to Austin as they walked behind Marvin Deck.

Hannah waited until Marvin Deck angrily sat in a chair near the TV, then asked, "How'd you get in here? We know you don't have a key."

Deck scowled and gripped the arms of his chair. "If you think I'm going to answer the questions of children, you're mistaken."

"Then we'll wait for Ezra Menski," Austin said gruffly as he sat on the sofa with Roxie beside him. The others sat wherever they could—on the couch and on the floor. "And he might even call the police and report you for breaking and entering."

Deck flushed and moved restlessly.

Just then the front door opened, and Emma and Ezra walked in. They stopped short when they saw Marvin Deck.

Austin jumped up and pointed to Deck. "We caught him in Lenny's study! He's Marvin Deck!"

Ezra chuckled dryly. "Well, well . . . We've been wanting to talk to you. I understand you wanted to buy some of Lenny's antiques."

Deck rose from his chair and tried to appear sure of himself. "Lenny said I could buy what I wanted!"

"I find that very hard to believe." Ezra grinned as he wrapped his hands around his suspenders. "I happen to know better. He gave some to Sue Monroe and wanted the rest sent to him."

"I don't believe it!"

Emma nodded. "We'll give him a call right now and get this settled."

Roxie felt proud of her grandma. She knew Lenny couldn't be reached by phone the whole weekend, but Marvin Deck didn't know that.

Deck cleared his throat. "That's not necessary."

"Because you're lying!" Ezra shook his finger at Deck. "Admit it!"

Deck shrugged. "Can't blame a man for trying."

"But we can blame a man for breaking into a house and stealing a box of antiques meant for someone else." Ezra's voice boomed across the room. "Unless you want to be prosecuted for stealing the items, return them immediately."

"I don't know what you're talking about."

Emma clicked her tongue. "We were in town this morning in your shop and saw the cranberry red pitcher Lenny planned to give to someone."

Deck crumpled and sank back to the chair. "You can't prove anything!"

"I'm sure we could, but we'll be satisfied with getting the things back that you took." Ezra named them off. "And we want them today!"

A muscle jumped in Deck's jaw. "I'll get them and be back."

"Before 3!"

Deck barely moved his head. "Before 3."

Emma opened the front door and stood there until Deck walked out. Ezra followed him. Emma hesitated, then hurried after him.

With the others talking behind her, Kathy walked to the window and looked out. She saw Marvin Deck hurrying down the driveway while Ezra and Emma stopped beside the station wagon. But she wasn't thinking about Deck or what he'd done. She was thinking about Roxie and how much she loved Austin. Roxie was sitting beside him on the sofa, looking as if someone had told her a wonderful secret. What would she do when she learned Austin and Bev were going together?

Chelsea sneaked a peek at Roxie too. How her face glowed! Chelsea's stomach turned over. She didn't want to think about how sad Roxie would be when she learned the truth.

Hannah also glanced at Roxie, then at Austin. Why was he acting as if he really liked Roxie when he was going with Bev? It wasn't right!

Roxie wanted to move closer to Austin until they were touching, but she couldn't find the courage. She'd hate to learn he didn't like her as much as she liked him. But surely he did or he wouldn't act the way he was acting.

"I can't believe Marvin Deck had the nerve to come in the house!" Austin jumped up and paced the floor. Suddenly he stopped and slapped his forehead. "We forgot to ask him if he found the hidden room!"

"He probably wouldn't have told us even if we'd asked," Kris said.

The door opened, and Ezra and Emma walked in. They looked at Austin and the girls. "He's gone," Ezra said. "He parked his car along the road so we wouldn't know he was here."

Emma set her purse on the TV. "I don't think Mr. Deck will sneak in again."

Ezra grinned. "I talked pretty straight to him. He doesn't want to end up in jail. Besides, he knows we have all the antiques packed and will be sending them to Lenny immediately."

"That's the end of our trouble with Marvin Deck," Emma said in relief.

Ezra sank down on the chair Deck had occupied. "After he brings the things back for Sue, we'll be well rid of him."

"Unless he wants to find the secret room." Hannah perched on the arm of the sofa. "He might think Lenny hid valuable things in there."

The others moaned.

"That's possible." Ezra crossed his long, bony legs and grinned. "But he better not try it."

Chelsea jumped up with a cry. "We forgot to tell you something really really important! We know the secret passage is in that closet." She pointed at it.

Her eyes flashing with excitement, Kathy nodded. "Roxie and I saw someone run in there, and when we looked he or she was gone! Gone!"

"Vanished!" Roxie cried.

"It could've been Bev Doanne," Austin said hoarsely.

Chelsea, Kathy, and Hannah heard the special way he said Bev's name. Anger rushed through them. They wanted to kick him out of the house, but they didn't say or do anything. They didn't want to hurt Roxie.

Roxie smiled at Austin. It was so cute of him to be that concerned about Bev Doanne. He really was a nice boy! As soon as she could get him alone, she'd tell him just how she felt about him.

Ezra hurried to the closet and looked inside. "I

can't believe it's in here. I've checked it over a million times."

"We'll check it two million times," Emma said softly as she walked around him into the closet.

Hannah, Chelsea, and Kathy peered into the closet. Was it possible they'd find the hidden passage in the next few minutes? They looked at each other and smiled, then glanced back at Roxie. She was too intent on Austin to think about the hidden room.

What would she do when she learned the truth?

11

The Awful Truth

Chelsea stepped back from the closet with a loud sigh. They'd taken turns inspecting the closet for the hidden passage and so far had found nothing. Why hadn't Lenny told someone? It was ridiculous to have a hidden passage and not tell anyone where it was. But then again, if you told someone, it wouldn't be a secret, would it? She was feeling very confused.

Hannah beckoned to Chelsea to join her near the open window. A pleasant breeze blew in fresh air. "Marvin Deck just drove in. Let's go ask him about the hidden room."

"What if he's mean to us?"

"We'll just scream."

Chelsea giggled. "We can do that all right."

Hannah slipped out the door with Chelsea right behind her. They wanted to see Deck alone so they could learn about the hidden room before anyone else did—if he knew about it.

Marvin Deck jerked the back door of his car open and lifted a box from the seat. He thrust it at Hannah. "Take it—and tell Menski to leave me alone." It was the box of things that belonged to Sue Monroe.

"He'll leave you alone as long as you stay away from here," Chelsea said with a flip of her fiery red hair.

"He said he wants you to forget you even know where the secret passage is. He'll see that it's locked so nobody can trespass." Hannah waited, barely breathing. Would Marvin Deck fall for the trap? She knew deep inside that she shouldn't be lying, but she sooo wanted to find the secret passage—and Bev.

Deck laughed. "So the old man finally discovered the tunnel. I thought he'd have to tear the shed down before he ever found it."

Hannah and Chelsea exchanged quick looks but kept themselves from looking shocked. So the secret passage led from the closet to the shed!

Hannah almost dropped the box in her excitement. She carefully set the box in the backseat of the station wagon, then turned back to Deck. "So you know there aren't any antiques hidden in the passage."

"Of course I know!"

"It's amazing anyone could think of such an

incredible way to open the door." Chelsea waited for Deck's answer. She and Hannah knew how easy it was to get answers if they pretended to already know them.

Deck nodded. "It took a real genius to design it."

"How did you ever find it?" Chelsea asked.

Deck shrugged. "Pure luck, I guess."

"Oh?" Hannah held her breath and waited for his answer.

"I stopped in one day to see Lenny Menski and he was heading for the shed, so I followed him. He was opening the hidden door when I stepped in." Deck chuckled dryly. "He was mad, I'll tell you. Mad! But it didn't do any good. I'd seen it."

Hannah glanced quickly at Chelsea, then back to Deck. "See if you can do it again, would you?"

"I could open it anytime!"

"Let's go."

Before they could move Ezra opened the door and shouted, "Get out of here, Deck! You brought the box—now leave!"

"Not yet!" Chelsea shouted.

"Right now," Ezra snapped.

Deck jerked open his car door, slid in, and roared away.

Hannah and Chelsea wanted to scream. They'd been sooo close to finding a way into the tunnel! How would they ever get in now? They turned to tell Ezra, but he'd gone back inside and closed the door.

Hannah squinted in the sunlight as she glanced toward the shed. "Let's check it out again."

"We know to look where it's free of cobwebs." Chelsea quickened her pace to keep up with Hannah.

"It's sooo frustrating to be so close to knowing the secret!" Hannah slid the door open with a vengeance. "How are we ever going to find the opening? We already looked it over before."

"But we didn't know for positive it was in here. Now we do."

Hannah rushed to the corner and studied it carefully. "Can you see anything, Chel?"

"I sure can't!" Chelsea peered at the wall and at the support post. "It's funny, isn't it?"

"What?"

"The answer's right in front of us, and we can't even see it." Thoughtfully Chelsea twisted the end of her hair around her finger. "It makes me think of my problems."

Hannah stopped searching to listen to Chelsea.

"I don't think I have an answer, but it's there all the time: trusting God. He has all the answers to everything. He wants me to spend time with Him— reading the Bible, praying, listening to Him. You understand, don't you, Hannah?"

"I sure do!" Hannah was thinking about the

help God had promised her in telling Mom about the pickle dish. She'd worried and worried about it when the answer was there all along: accept courage and help from her Heavenly Father so she could tell Mom the truth. She told Chelsea her thoughts. "I made something easy into a giant task."

"Me too!" Chelsea grinned sheepishly. "I've been really scared to talk to Mr. Borgman about that terrible book. Why be scared? With help from the Lord, I'll tell him what I need to tell him. It's as simple as that!"

Hannah rubbed the wall. "Let's pray that God will help us find the way into the secret passage."

Chelsea nodded.

They bowed their heads together—black against red. Hannah prayed, "Heavenly Father, thank You for helping us all the time with every single problem we have. Show us the way into the secret passage."

Chelsea added, "And show us how to help Bev and her mom and sister if they're hiding here or are somewhere else. Let them know You love them and are watching over them. In Jesus' name, Amen."

They smiled at each other and started looking again for the hidden door. A sudden sound behind them made them jump.

"It's just us," Kathy said with a laugh as she and Roxie walked in.

"Grandma sent us to look for you." Roxie

sighed dreamily. "I didn't want to leave Austin, but I did anyway."

"I made her come." Kathy bit her lower lip. It wasn't going to be easy, but they had to tell Roxie the truth about Bev and Austin before Roxie fell even deeper in love.

Hannah and Chelsea knew why Kathy had brought Roxie. None of them wanted to break Roxie's heart, but she had to know the truth—broken heart or not. Silently they prayed for the right words to say.

Roxie backed away, suddenly feeling very uncomfortable. "Why are you all looking at me that way?"

Hannah took a deep breath. "We have something to tell you."

"It'll make you feel bad," Kathy whispered.

Tears stung Chelsea's eyes. "We have to do it because we love you."

The color drained from Roxie's face. "What is it? No!" She held up her hands as if to ward off a blow. "Don't tell me! I don't want to know."

"We have to tell you." Hannah looked from Kathy to Chelsea. She could see by their faces they wanted *her* to tell Roxie. "It's . . . about Austin."

Roxie frowned. "Austin? What about him?"

Hannah's mouth turned dry. Could she say it? Yes! She had to, for Roxie's sake. "He and Bev Doanne go together."

Roxie shook her head. "No . . . No."

"It's true."

"It can't be!"

"Kris and Heather said so."

"They told us today, but they thought we already knew," Chelsea said.

"It's not a secret." Kathy wanted to wrap her arms around Roxie and hold her tight, but she didn't move. Roxie wouldn't want a hug right now.

"But why is he acting like he likes me?" Roxie's voice broke, and she gulped.

"He probably does like you," Kathy said. "But he's going with Bev. He might think you know it already."

Roxie shook her head as tears welled up in her eyes. "Are you really *really* sure?"

"Yes," they said together.

"No! It just can't be!" Hot tears rolled down Roxie's cheeks.

"Let the Holy Spirit comfort you," Hannah whispered. "You know the Bible says the Holy Spirit was sent as our Comforter."

Roxie turned and ran from the shed and headed for the woods. She couldn't face anyone right now, not even the Best Friends. Sobs tore from her throat. How could she survive? The pain was worse than any she'd ever felt in her entire life.

She ran into the shade of the woods and down the path. Suddenly she tripped on a tree root and sprawled to the ground. She lay there and sobbed into the fallen leaves.

The Best Friends slowly followed Roxie into the woods. They knew that when she'd finished crying she would want them to be with her. Best friends needed each other during a crisis.

They finally found her lying on the ground. They quietly sat beside her. They silently prayed for her because they knew God answered prayer.

Suddenly Jim Doanne stepped into sight. His face was white as he stared down at Roxie. "What's wrong?"

The Best Friends leaped up. Roxie was crying too hard to hear and stayed where she was.

"What's wrong with her?" Jim asked again.

"She heard some bad news," Hannah said in a low voice so she wouldn't disturb Roxie.

Jim rubbed an unsteady hand over his face. "About Bev?"

"No." Chelsea shook her head. "Well, kind of."

Jim leaned weakly against an oak. "Is Bev hurt?"

Hannah frowned. "We don't know. We haven't seen her."

"Then what are you talking about?"

Kathy faced Jim Doanne squarely. "Roxie likes Austin Coltrain, the boy Bev goes with."

"I didn't know Bev went with a boy." Jim

Doanne pushed away from the oak. "She never told me."

"Maybe you were too busy beating her," Chelsea snapped.

Jim's eyes widened in alarm. "Who told you that? It's not true! I don't beat her!"

Just then Roxie heard voices around her. She lifted her tear-stained face, then brushed self-consciously at her eyes. She'd heard Jim Doanne's exclamation. She sat up and shouted, "Oh, yes, you do! You probably made her cry a lot harder than I just did!"

Jim turned away, his head down and his shoulders bent. Without another word he walked back into the woods.

The Best Friends squatted down beside Roxie. "Are you okay?"

Roxie shook her head.

They lifted her to her feet and all hugged her at the same time. She smelled like pine needles and old leaves.

Later they slowly walked back to the yard. Roxie stopped beside the shed. "I can't face Austin yet. I'll stay in the shed to look for the opening. Tell Grandma."

"We will," Hannah said gently.

"I'll stay with you." Kathy smiled at Roxie. "Is that all right?"

"Sure. Thanks."

Smiling, Hannah and Chelsea headed for the house. They would have to hurry if they were to find the secret passage before it was time to go home. But they'd find it—somehow.

12

Locked In

Hannah stopped Chelsea outside the front door of Lenny's house. "Chel, you know we can't treat Austin bad just because he paid attention to Roxie."

Chelsea knotted her fists and glared at the door as if she could see right through it to Austin. "I feel like telling him just what I think of him!"

"But you won't, will you?"

Chelsea wrinkled her nose. "No . . . I guess I won't."

"And I won't either. He probably didn't try to make Roxie fall for him."

"You're right, I guess." Chelsea opened the door. With God's help she'd be nice to Austin.

As they walked in, Ezra stepped out of the closet with a scowl on his face. "I don't know why we can't find the opening! Are you girls sure it's there?" His gaze fell on Hannah and Chelsea. "Where's Roxann?"

"And Kathy," Emma added.

"They're in the shed." Hannah told them what they'd learned from Marvin Deck.

Ezra helplessly shook his head. "I wish I'd known that when he was here. He wouldn't show us now if we paid him."

Austin glanced at his watch. "We can't stay much longer. I'm going to try to find the entrance again." He disappeared inside the closet and thumped here and there on the back wall.

Emma perched on the arm of the sofa. "I called Sue Monroe to tell her we have her gifts from Lenny, but there was no answer. I'll try again in a few minutes."

Hannah and Chelsea left Emma and Ezra talking as they joined Austin in the closet. Kris and Heather soon followed. It made the closet crowded, but they wanted to find the opening too much to care.

"Maybe we'll have to chop a hole in the wall," Hannah said with a grin.

"I feel like it!" Austin thumped the wall with his fist. "What if Bev's in there and can't get out?"

"Whoever's in there knows the way out." Chelsea rested her hand on a hook. "Don't let that frighten you."

Kris cleared her throat. "I just had a terrible thought. What if Bev is in there and what if someone is holding her a prisoner?"

Hannah shivered, then squared her shoulders.

"We prayed for Bev. No matter what the situation is, God will take care of her!"

Across the yard in the shed Roxie and Kathy leaned against the wall as they tried to think of where else they could look for the hidden opening.

Roxie crossed her arms and scowled. "It seems hopeless."

"We sure didn't expect any of this when we came to help Ezra." Kathy giggled. "But it does make it exciting."

"I guess so." Roxie bit her lip. Right now nothing seemed exciting.

Just then the wall they leaned on moved. They screamed, but before they could jump away and get their balance they stumbled and fell back onto a dirt floor. Then, before they could move, Bev Doanne slipped into the shed and closed the hidden door, leaving the two Best Friends on the wrong side of the wall.

"Hey!" Kathy jumped to her feet. "Come back!"

"That was Bev Doanne!"

"I know." Kathy looked around with interest. The light from a nearby lantern cast a glow to show a narrow passageway and wooden steps leading down. "Roxie, the shed has a false wall!"

Slowly Roxie stood, her legs trembling so badly she didn't know if she could stand. "Let's get out of here!"

"Not yet." Kathy lifted the lantern high. She

smelled kerosene from the lantern and felt the
packed dirt they stood on. "Let's follow the tunnel
and see where it leads."

"Are you kidding? I want out of here!" Roxie
pounded on the wall. "Let us out right now!" She
began to sweat like crazy. Her fists hurt from hitting
the wooden wall so hard. "Open this door!"

Kathy caught Roxie's arm. "Calm down! Look
around you. We wanted to find the tunnel and here
we are."

"I'm scared."

"But why?"

"What if we never get out?"

"We will. Even if Ezra has to knock out a wall
to find us, he'll get us out of here. You know Ezra.
He never gives up."

Roxie laughed weakly. "You're right about
that." She sighed and slowly surveyed the scene. "I
guess we could look around."

"I wonder why Bev ran out and left us in here?
Now she doesn't have a hiding place from her dad."

"Maybe she decided to go home where she
belongs."

"Maybe." Kathy wasn't convinced of that, but
right now she wanted to explore. "Ready to go?"

"I guess. But don't walk fast!"

"I won't. We'll stay together." Kathy held the
lantern away from her as she slowly, carefully
walked down the wooden steps. There was a dirt

wall on either side. At the bottom of the steps she saw a tunnel stretching out in front of them with a dirt floor, sides, and ceiling and beams to keep the tunnel from collapsing. Sand filtered down, making a funny noise as it did. "Just think, Roxie! Slaves once used this very tunnel!"

"I can't think about anything but getting out of here." Roxie shivered, then sneezed. "Shouldn't we be at the house by now? What if the tunnel takes us clear to Canada?"

Kathy laughed. "It can't."

"Maybe it goes right into town."

"Roxie, we haven't been walking that long." Kathy stopped and listened. All she heard was their breathing and gently falling sand. "Doesn't it feel strange not to hear other people or cars on the highway or birds?"

Roxie whimpered. "Please *please* keep going!"

"I wonder how long the slaves had to stay in here before it was safe for them to go to the next station."

"Kathy!"

"I sure am glad I didn't live back then and that I'm not a slave."

"Will you get going?"

"I wonder how Bev stood it down here."

Roxie jabbed Kathy in the back. "Let's get out of here! Right now!"

"All right! It's not as if we're in any danger."

Kathy began walking again. "Even our voices hit the walls and ceiling and go no farther. It's weird."

"Can you walk faster, Kathy? I can't breathe."

"Just relax and breathe normally. You'll be okay."

"No. It's the dirt. It's choking me."

Kathy walked a little faster with Roxie on her heels. Finally they reached a flight of wooden steps leading up. Kathy hesitated, and Roxie bumped into her.

"Shall we go back or go up?" Kathy trembled, making the lantern jump and the shadows dance.

"Up, of course! I want back above ground before I turn into a mole."

Chuckling, Kathy walked up the steep flight of wooden steps and through a door into a tiny room. Blankets were stacked against a wall with a sack of garbage beside them. She saw the empty marshmallow bag and empty pop cans. "Somebody has been living here for sure," she whispered.

Roxie stared in horror at the pile of blankets. "How awful!"

"It was probably Bev and her mom and sister. I wonder how long they've been hiding out?"

"Almost a week," Bev said behind them.

Roxie and Kathy shrieked in surprise. "Bev!"

She stepped forward. "I didn't know you knew we were here."

Roxie scowled at Bev. Her hair was in tangles,

and she smelled as if she hadn't taken a shower in days. How could Austin love her?

"We thought you ran away just now and weren't coming back to get us out," Kathy said.

"I had to go to the bathroom. Then I followed you through the tunnel and back here into the secret room. It wasn't easy." Bev pushed her hands into the pockets of her pants. Her jeans and yellow blouse were stained and dirty, as though she'd lived in the same clothes a long time—which she had. "Mom and Alexa went out the shed entrance a while ago and haven't returned. Did you see them anywhere?"

"No, but we saw your dad."

Bev groaned. "Oh no! I hope he didn't find them and force them to go home with him."

"Austin told us about him beating you," Kathy said softly.

Bev gasped. "How'd Austin know? I never told him!"

"He probably saw the bruises."

Roxie knotted her fists. She couldn't hold back the dreaded question a minute longer. "Are you going with Austin?"

Bev nodded. "I thought about breaking up with him because of . . . because of Dad." Bev looked down at the dusty wooden floor, then up at the girls. "I know it's my fault he beats us, and I told him I'll try to be the perfect daughter he wants. I don't know if it helped."

Kathy didn't know what to say to that. She knew it couldn't be Bev's fault, but she didn't think Bev would believe her. "Does your grandma know you're here?"

Bev nodded. "Lenny Menski showed her the secret room a long time ago, so when we needed a place to stay, Grandma brought us here."

"What'll you do when the new owners move in?"

"I hope we can go home. But Mom won't until Dad gets help."

"Ezra will help," Kathy said.

Roxie scowled. What could *he* do? He was gruff and mean himself.

Bev took the lantern from Kathy and set it on the floor. "Before Friday we slept in the beds and used the kitchen and the bathrooms. We even watched TV. It was like having a home of our own, only without Dad. We couldn't use it after you came. It's been kind of . . . hard. You almost caught me twice."

Kathy's eyes widened. "Were you the one who was using the phone?"

"Yes. I was trying to convince Dad I'd be good. He wouldn't listen any more than when I tried before."

As Bev and Kathy talked, Roxie looked around to see where the door was that led into the closet. She couldn't see it. Panic rose in her, and she tried to hold it down. "Open the door so we can leave, will you?"

Bev shook her head. "I can't until Mom and Alexa come back."

"What?" Roxie's voice rose, but Bev quickly clamped her mouth shut.

"You could let us out in the shed, and nobody would know we saw you or talked to you," Kathy said. She didn't want to be a prisoner in the hidden room, and she knew Roxie felt the same way.

Bev shook her head. "Please don't ask me to. I just can't be alone in here!"

"But the others will worry about us." Kathy started past Bev to knock on the wall, but Bev tugged her back.

"Don't! I mean it."

Kathy and Roxie stared at Bev in alarm. She was serious! She wasn't going to let them go!

■

Meanwhile, in the shed Chelsea and Hannah looked all around. "Where are they?" they both asked at once.

"Do you think they found a way inside?" Chelsea shuddered just thinking of the girls being in the passage all by themselves.

Hannah shook her head. "They would've told us if they'd gotten the door opened. I know they would've!"

"Then where are they? Would Jim Doanne force them to go with him?"

"I don't think so." Hannah walked outdoors in the glaring sunshine and looked all around. "Maybe they got tired of looking."

"They would've gone in the house."

Hannah sighed heavily. "You're right. But where are they? I don't like this one bit!"

Chelsea cupped her hands around her mouth and shouted, "Roxie! Kathy! Can you hear me?" She waited, listening intently. All she heard was a truck on the highway and a blue jay in the woods.

"We have to find them before something terrible happens to them!" Hannah shielded her eyes and looked toward the woods, then at the barn, and finally inside the shed again. "Roxie! Kathy! Where are you?"

Chelsea wrapped her arms protectively around herself. "We'd better tell Emma and Ezra."

Hannah nodded. They stood side by side and stared at the area of the shed where they knew the secret door was hidden. Silently they prayed for Roxie and Kathy.

"They have angels watching over them," Hannah whispered. "They'll be okay."

13

Rescued

In the hidden room Roxie glared down at Bev. "You have to let us out right now!"

Kathy secretly agreed with Roxie, but she didn't want to say anything that might upset Bev even more. She was already upset enough. In the last few minutes she'd burst into tears without any warning. "Bev, we want to help you. But we can't if we're locked up inside here."

Bev wrung her hands and looked ready to cry again. "I just don't know what to do. Why haven't Mom and Alexa come back? Would they leave me here all alone?"

"Of course not." Kathy knelt down on the dirty floor and put an arm around Bev. "You have help now. You're no longer alone. Your grandma's helping you, and so are we, and Ezra and Emma Menski are too. And we're all praying for you."

"Dad will be really really angry that so many people know he beats us."

Roxie's jaw tightened. How could a dad beat his own kids? And even his wife!

"Now maybe he'll get help so he can stop doing it." Kathy leaned her forehead against Bev's dirty hair. It smelled like the dusty room. "Wouldn't you like to live without his anger and without him beating you?"

"It's hard to imagine it any different."

"But it will be!"

Roxie leaned down to Bev and Kathy. "Bev, please open the door and let us out. I can't breathe in here with all this dirt."

Bev's lip quivered. "When Mom and Alexa come, then I'll let you out."

Roxie sank to the floor and moaned.

■

In the living room Chelsea and Hannah told the others that Roxie and Kathy had disappeared. They were all upset, and everyone talked at once until Ezra put a stop to it with a gruff command: "QUIET!"

"We looked all over," Hannah said.

"And we called and called them." Chelsea looked ready to cry.

"You're sure they're in the hidden passage?" Austin asked sharply.

Hannah barely nodded.

Chelsea spread her hands wide. "Where else could they be? They'd have answered us by now if they were in the yard or the woods."

"This is serious." Emma looked out the window, then turned back to the others. "If we don't find them within the next few minutes, we'll call their parents."

"We'll find them." Ezra hugged Emma close. "God is with us—and with them."

■

A few minutes later Hannah and Chelsea ran outside just in time to see Sue Monroe dressed in jeans and a lavender sweater creeping toward the shed, and they quickly ducked behind a tall lilac bush. A startled robin flew from its nest and on up to a tall maple. The girls watched Sue slip inside, and then they raced to the door and peeked in. Sue stood near the corner and pushed against a support post. The wall opened, and she stepped into the secret passageway. It closed silently behind her.

"That's amazing!" Hannah whispered.

"Thank God! Now we know the way in." Chelsea ran to the post and reached to push it.

"Wait!" Hannah caught Chelsea's arm. "It's dark in there. We'll need a flashlight."

"Ezra has one in the station wagon. I'll get it." Chelsea ran to the door, then stopped short. "Hannah, come quick! Look!" Chelsea pointed at the woods.

"What?" Hannah joined her and looked to where she was pointing. "I see something yellow. What is it?"

"I saw Jim Doanne with someone with a yellow shirt, but they stepped out of sight before you could see them. I wonder if he has Bev."

"This is awful! We have to get Ezra!" Hannah dashed to the house with Chelsea right beside her.

■

In the hidden room Roxie paced back and forth. The longer she was locked in, the smaller the room seemed to get. She heard Bev and Kathy talking where they sat on the floor, but she didn't listen to them. She wanted out!

Just then she caught a flash of light on the stairs. Her fingers stung with fear. She dropped beside Bev and Kathy and pointed with a shaky finger.

Kathy's mouth turned as dry as the dust on the floor.

Bev froze. She knew her mom and sister didn't have a light. Had they found one, or was it someone else coming to get them? Was it her dad?

"Mallary . . . Alexa . . . Bev . . . it's me." Sue Monroe came right behind the flash of light. The smell of her perfume filled the space.

"Grandma!"

Sue cried out in shock when she saw Roxie and Kathy there. "Bev, what are they doing in here?"

Bev quickly explained, then asked, "Do you know where Mom and Alexa are?"

"No!" Sue sank to the floor, and the light from the flashlight danced wildly on the wall and ceiling. "When did they leave here?"

Bev told her. "But they should've been back long ago. I didn't know what to do. Roxie and Kathy want to leave, but I couldn't let them go yet."

"You have to," Kathy said softly.

Roxie bit back an angry comment. She knew neither anger nor fear would persuade Bev—she had already tried both.

Sue slowly stood. "Girls, you'll have to wait a little longer. When Mallary and Alexa are here safely, then you can go. Not before."

"But what if they never come back?" Roxie's voice seemed to fill the small space. She was sure it had carried to the closet. Maybe Austin would come crashing through and save her. But he wouldn't save her—he'd save Bev instead!

Kathy patted Roxie's arm. "We'll be all right. God is with us, remember?"

■

Outdoors a few minutes later Hannah and Chelsea watched Ezra and Austin walk silently into the woods. They heard an angry voice and knew it was Jim Doanne.

"I want to go with Ezra," Chelsea whispered.

"Me too, but we have to follow Sue Monroe to see if Roxie and Kathy are in the secret room."

Chelsea threw up her hands. "I want to do it all!"

Hannah giggled. "Me too, but we can't." They really didn't have a choice—saving best friends always came first.

They hurried to the corner of the shed and pushed where Sue had pushed. The wall opened, and Hannah clicked on the flashlight and stepped inside. The wall closed behind them, and they grabbed each other fearfully.

"Now how do we get out?" Chelsea whispered.

Hannah flashed the light over the wall. The color drained from her face. "I don't know. I thought it would be easy to get out."

"Are we . . . locked in just like we were locked out?"

Hannah barely nodded. Then she smiled. "But wait! Sue Monroe's in here. She knows the way out."

Chelsea sagged in relief. "I'd forgotten."

"Let's go." Hannah led the way down the stairs to the underground tunnel. She wrinkled her nose. She'd hate to live underground. "I'd hate to be in here more than a few minutes."

"Me too! I feel like a snake or something!"

"Or a mole."

"Or a groundhog."

"Or a rabbit."

The girls giggled as they walked. Giggling was better than shivering with fear—the thing they both fought against.

Finally they reached another stair. They looked at each other with the same question inside their heads: should they continue? They nodded at the same time.

Slowly they crept up the stairs. They heard voices and stopped. Would they find Roxie and Kathy with Sue Monroe? Was Bev there too?

Hannah clicked off the flashlight, and they stood in the darkness, then slowly, silently crept up the steps with their hands on the dirt walls to keep their balance. The voices grew louder until they could understand what was being said.

"We want out right now!" Roxie said firmly.

"They must've noticed we're missing." Kathy's voice faltered. "You can't keep us here much longer."

"I know." Sue Monroe sounded tired. "Bev, she's right—we can't. We have to find Mallary and Alexa before your father does."

Hannah clicked on her flashlight and said, "We think he already did."

Bev cried out as Roxie and Kathy rushed at Hannah and Chelsea.

When the greetings were over, Sue Monroe demanded an explanation.

"We saw you open the secret door in the shed." Hannah flashed her light around the tiny room as she spoke. It felt crowded and almost airless with all of them crammed together. "Before we could get a flashlight to follow you, we saw Jim Doanne with someone in the woods. We told Ezra, and he's out there right now taking care of it."

"Jim might hit him! I have to get out there immediately!" Sue pushed a spot on the wall, and the closet door pivoted. Light and fresh air rushed in as Sue forced her way out. The closet was empty. No sounds came from other parts of the house.

Hannah grabbed a blanket and stuffed it in just the right spot so the door couldn't accidentally close. She tugged Bev out with her, and the others followed.

"Let me go!" Bev wrenched free and sped out the front door after her grandma.

The Best Friends looked at each other, then hugged each other at the same time. They looked like football players in a huddle. Finally they broke apart.

"Let's find the others," Kathy said as she headed for the door.

"And see what's happening with Jim Doanne and Ezra." Roxie laughed. "I'd hate to be Jim Doanne once Ezra gets ahold of him."

The girls ran outdoors into the bright sunlight and the fabulous fresh air. They breathed deeply, then ran toward the woods.

14

The Perfect Answer

In the woods Roxie stopped short when she caught sight of Austin. Oh, but she loved him! And he loved Bev. Life was not fair!

The Best Friends looked back and saw that Roxie had stopped. They ran to her and stood with her to face her agony. The bright red, orange, gold, and yellow leaves blocked out the warm sun. They wished they could block out Roxie's pain as efficiently.

Sue and Bev ran to Mallary and Alexa where they clung together under a tall yellow maple. Emma, Kris, and Heather stood nearby, ready to help if needed.

Ezra held Jim Doanne by the arm. "You have to face the truth, Jim!"

"Let me go! I'll have you jailed for this."

"No, you won't." Ezra lowered his voice. "You

don't want the whole state to know what you've done."

Austin spotted Bev and walked toward her, a relieved smile on his face.

Roxie looked away. She couldn't watch Austin hug Bev.

Bev pulled away from her family and ran to meet Austin. She hugged him tightly. "Thanks for being here for me."

"Sure. I wish I could help with your dad, but he won't listen to me at all."

"I think he's listening to Ezra Menski though." Bev smiled briefly, then walked back to her family, her hand securely in Austin's. They stood side by side and watched Ezra and Jim Doanne.

Suddenly Jim Doanne broke away from Ezra. "Leave me alone, old man! There's nothing you can say to me that I'll listen to."

The Best Friends gasped. For a minute they thought Jim was going to strike Ezra.

With a cry Mallary ran to Ezra's side and faced Jim squarely. Her face was red, and she trembled. "Jim, don't you dare hit him!"

"He's butting in where he's not wanted."

"He's helping us. Unless you get help to stop your rages, the girls and I are leaving you for good. We will no longer put up with your abuse."

"Do you think I want to hit you? Or the girls? I don't! But you make me."

Bev pulled free from Austin and ran to her dad and flung her arms around him. "I told you I'd be a good daughter. I mean it!"

Mallary walked right up to Jim and pulled Bev away, holding her close. "You're already a good daughter, Bev. And he still beats us. Alexa is a good daughter, and I'm a good wife." She pointed her finger at Jim. "*You* are the one to blame! Not us! You lose control because of something inside you, not because of what we do or say."

"She's right," Ezra said gruffly.

"What do you know, old man?" Jim stormed away, right toward the Best Friends. They scattered out of his way. He caught Roxie by the arm, almost lifting her off her feet. He turned to face Ezra. "I know this is your granddaughter. You tell my family to come home with me right now or I'll break her arm."

Roxie's heart zoomed to her feet, and the color drained from her face.

The Best Friends stood helplessly by. If they moved, he might just do what he'd said. Silently they prayed for help.

"Don't do it, Dad!" Bev burst into wild tears. "Please don't hurt her! I'll go home with you."

"Mallary? Alexa?" Jim's face was dark with anger.

They stepped forward as tears streamed down their cheeks.

"Stop!" Ezra walked right up to Jim. Ezra was half a head taller than Jim, but Jim seemed to tower over him. Ezra bent his head and looked Jim right in the eyes. "You will not hurt her. Let her go *now*."

"Who's going to make me?"

"You are! You've hurt enough people, and you've been hurt enough yourself."

Jim slowly released Roxie. "I'm sorry . . . So sorry."

Roxie ran into her grandma's arms, shivering uncontrollably.

The Best Friends ran to her and patted her arms and spoke soothingly to her.

Ezra clamped his hand on Jim's shoulder. "I know where you can get good counsel so you can have control of your emotions."

"Tell me," Jim whispered.

Ezra did. "And I know the perfect answer for you. It's God. Jesus loves you. He wants to be your Savior."

"I don't know . . ."

"We'll get together and talk. I'll show you in the Bible just how much God cares for you and your family." Ezra smiled. "You're not alone, Jim. Not any more."

"Thanks." Jim's voice broke, and he couldn't go on.

The Best Friends smiled happily. Things were

going to be just fine! Maybe not everything would be OK right away, but in time . . .

Later Sue Monroe took Mallary and the girls home with her until they could move back in with Jim. And Jim drove away with the name and address of the man Ezra had suggested and a promise to meet with Ezra regularly for prayer and Bible study.

Austin, Kris, and Heather said good-bye and rode their bikes toward home.

Roxie watched until Austin was out of sight. Her heart ached, but she'd survived. After all, she still had her best friends.

Later, in the house after everything was clean again and the secret door in the closet was closed, Roxie walked to the kitchen where Ezra sat with a cup of coffee. The aroma drifted across the room.

Ezra lifted his shaggy brow and studied her. "What?"

She almost turned and ran. She'd wanted to ask the Best Friends to go with her, but she knew this was something she had to do on her own. "Thank you for saving me from Jim Doanne."

Ezra shrugged.

"You weren't even afraid of him, and he's lots younger than you."

Ezra chuckled. "I have help from God. I didn't have to fear."

"You didn't? Sometimes I get really scared." Roxie flushed. "Over a lot of things."

"Roxann, you don't have to keep fear inside you. But I think you know that, don't you? God didn't give you a spirit of fear."

Her eyes widened. "I know that Bible verse! It's Kathy's favorite—it's 2 Timothy 1:7."

Ezra nodded. "That's right. God gave you a spirit of power and love and a sound mind, not fear." Ezra caught Roxie's hand and held it gently in his big, bony hand. "When fear tries to take control of you, you just kick it out in the name of Jesus. He is more powerful than the fear. It must obey and leave you."

Roxie shivered. "I don't know."

"Sure you do. You're learning to obey God's Word, aren't you?"

"Yes."

"Telling fear to leave you is being obedient to God. Want me to help you kick fear out?"

Roxie's eyes widened. She'd never thought of Ezra doing such a thing. Finally she nodded.

Ezra put his hand on Roxie's head and said, "Fear, in the name of Jesus you must leave Roxann! You have no place in her. Jesus, fill her with love and peace and a sound mind. Thank You."

Roxie smiled. She felt the peace inside where before she'd felt fear about everything. She could probably even walk through the secret tunnel without shivering and shaking! Why, she could even give the speech in school Monday that she'd been too afraid to think about or talk about.

"You're a fine granddaughter, Roxann."

"Thanks." She stepped back a ways and studied Ezra. She'd never wanted to admit to being his granddaughter before. It sounded really nice. "What should I call you—Ezra or Grandpa?"

"Grandpa. That's who I am."

"Grandpa." Roxie rolled it around on her tongue. It felt good.

Later in the yard, while Ezra and Emma were taking another stroll around the place, Roxie told the Best Friends about her talk with Ezra. "If I forget to call him Grandpa, please remind me."

"We will."

Hannah chuckled. "I hate to say I told you so, but . . ."

"But you will," Roxie said with a laugh.

"I told you he was nice."

"I'm glad I found out."

"I can't believe it!" Chelsea pulled a paper from her back pocket. "I forgot to give this work sheet to Bev!"

"She doesn't need it," Kathy said. "She and I talked about the book and the class. She's not going to read it, and she said she'd talk to Mrs. Evans and Mr. Borgman with us."

"Good for her!" Chelsea pushed the work sheet back into her pocket. "When I get home I'll throw it away along with mine."

The Best Friends all turned at the same time and looked at the huge house with the hidden tunnel.

"This has been a fun two days," Kathy said.

Roxie nodded. "Even with Austin. I know now we can be friends even though he's going with Bev."

Chelsea faced Hannah. "This has been such a good two days, I vote we call this job our good deed for the *King's Kids*." Chelsea looked from Kathy to Roxie. "All in favor say yes."

"Yes!"

"Yes!"

"Yes!"

"Yes!"

"We all learned so much while we were here," Hannah said.

"We sure did!" Roxie yanked Chelsea's hair. "I told you that no matter how our talks start out, we always end up having a meeting."

Chelsea flipped back her red hair. "This meeting is adjourned. And so is our time in the country."

The Best Friends raced to the station wagon. Their laughter rang across the yard and on into the woods.

"I beat you all," Kathy said as she slipped into the backseat. "I'm the winner."

"We're all winners because of Jesus!" they cried. They all looked at each other and laughed. "And we're all best friends forever!"

You are invited to become a *Best Friends Member!*

In becoming a member you'll receive a club membership card with your name on the front and a list of the Best Friends and their favorite Bible verses on the back along with a space for your favorite Scripture. You'll also receive a colorful, 2-inch, specially-made I'M A BEST FRIEND button and a write-up about the author, Hilda Stahl, with her autograph. As a bonus you'll get an occasional newsletter about the upcoming BEST FRIENDS books.

All you need to do is mail your NAME, ADDRESS (printed neatly, please), AGE and $3.00 for postage and handling to:

BEST FRIENDS
P.O. Box 96
Freeport, MI 49325

WELCOME TO THE CLUB!

(Authorized by the author, Hilda Stahl)

Whyte Ridge Baptist Church
201 Scurfield Blvd.
Winnipeg, MB.   R3Y 1A5